'**What we nee** [...]
romance.'

Jennet gazed blankly [...] man who had stridden back into the room.

'Excuse me?'

'That's right.' Connor fixed pale grey eyes intently on hers. 'A red-hot encounter, full of joyous sexual abandon and free-floating lust.'

Jennet sat immobilised, her mind awhirl. Had he realised that she always slept alone?

'This is a joke!'

'I'm not joking. I'm deadly serious,' Connor said, his sober expression verifying his words.

Connor Malone believed in decisive actions. If he wanted something he went for it with a steely determination; and was invariably successful. Her heart pounded.

Elizabeth Oldfield's writing career started as a teenage hobby, when she had articles published. However, on her marriage the creative instinct was diverted into the production of a daughter and son. A decade later, when her husband's job took them to Singapore, she resumed writing and had her first romance accepted in 1982. Now hooked on the genre, she produces an average of three books a year. They live in London, and Elizabeth travels widely to authenticate the background of her books.

Recent titles by the same author:

INTIMATE RELATIONS
HIS SLEEPING PARTNER
LOOKING AFTER DAD

SOLUTION: SEDUCTION!

BY
ELIZABETH OLDFIELD

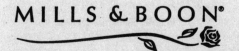
MILLS & BOON®

*First published in Great Britain 1997
Harlequin Mills & Boon Limited,
Eton House, 18-24 Paradise Road, Richmond, Surrey TW9 1SR*

© Elizabeth Oldfield 1997

ISBN 0 263 80146 2

*Set in Times Roman 10 on 12 pt.
01-9706-51020 C1*

*Printed and bound in Great Britain
by Mackays of Chatham PLC, Chatham*

CHAPTER ONE

'WHAT we need is to have a romance.'

Dragging her eyes away from the newspaper article which she was reading, Jennet gazed blankly at the tall, dark-haired man who had stridden back into the room.

'Excuse me?' she said as she closed the paper and hastily attempted to reassemble her thoughts.

The article had been unsettling. Would the appeal made in that final paragraph draw any response? she wondered. Were amateur detectives in the process of winkling out clues? Might gossipy informants have already jammed the switchboard? A chill shivered involuntarily down her spine. She hoped not.

'I reckon it's time we began a love affair,' Connor Malone declared, walking across the white cord-carpeted floor towards a bubbling expresso machine.

He indicated the mug which sat beside her on the polished ebony table. 'Want a fill-up?'

'Uh—yes, please.' She swigged the remaining half inch of gone-cold coffee. 'Black, one sugar.'

'No sign of Lester?' he asked as he diverted his long stride towards her.

''Fraid not.'

A meeting had been arranged. They had both arrived on time at the stipulated nine-thirty, but ten o'clock was approaching and Lester Sewell, founder and chairman of the Ensign television company, had yet to put in an appearance.

After waiting a while in the spacious fourth-floor office with its chic black and white decor, lurid examples of abstract art and bank of flat twenty-nine-inch state-of-the-art television screens, her companion had grown impatient. The day's heavy workload meant he had neither the time nor the inclination to hang around.

'There're a couple of matters which require my attention,' he had said, excusing himself, and had gone off to dictate strategy to one or other of his minions.

Left alone, Jennet had poured herself a coffee. She had checked through the papers in her bulky folder, placed roller-ball pen and notepad at the ready, then taken out the copy of the newspaper which the postman had pushed through her letterbox minutes before she had left the house that morning.

'A love affair?' she repeated, thinking she must have misheard.

No, the appeal would be ignored. The paper was small-town and local. Its readers were farmers, matronly stalwarts of the Women's Institute, people trawling the 'for sale' columns in the hope of spotting a bargain-priced second-hand car. They would skim the article at best, and promptly forget about it.

'That's right.' As he reached down to clasp long fingers around the mug, Connor fixed pale grey eyes intently on hers. 'What we need is a red-hot encounter, full of joyous sexual abandon and free-floating lust.'

Jennet blinked. It was fortunate she was sitting down, otherwise she might well have fallen down in a dead faint, she thought bemusedly—or needed something rock-solid to cling onto.

As the writer of a television comedy/drama which had drawn rave reviews on its debut run, she had been working in conjunction with Connor Malone, the director of the series, for almost a year now. During that time they had established a rapport, yet she had believed it to be a working rapport. Pure and simple. Nothing more. She had not realised she appealed to him on a personal basis and it had certainly never occurred to her that he might wish them to embark on an intimate physical liaison.

'Free—' Her mouth had gone dry and she needed to swallow. 'Free-floating lust?' she echoed chokily.

'It'd add one hell of a kick.'

As he strode over to operate the flow of hot coffee, Jennet sat immobilised, her mind awhirl. Although she had made only sparse reference to her private life, Connor would know she was a widow and lived alone. Had he realised that she always slept alone? Could he have guessed there were times, increasingly, when the lack of lovemaking made her feel restless and edgy? How she had begun to fantasise about nights of wild passion with dynamic-hipped strangers? It seemed possible. The director might not possess mind-reading powers, but he was remarkably astute and alert.

Suspicion narrowed her green eyes. Was this some kind of sneaky masculine assault on her vulnerability? Had he recognised what today's jargon would call 'a window of opportunity'—a *widow* of opportunity, a ho-ho voice adjusted in her head—and decided to take advantage? Did he expect her to fall at his feet in a blubbering mass of gratitude and thank him for rescuing her from her fate? Or start tearing away her clothes and offering herself up in eager sacrifice? If so, he had miscalculated.

'Maybe,' she said crisply, 'but I don't think that—'

'Why not?' he demanded.

'Because—' Jennet bounced a palm off her brow in an abrupt 'what an idiot!' gesture. 'This is a joke!' she said, and laughed. Laughed with deep-throated, gurgling relief. 'Sorry to be so slow on the uptake, but I was up at the crack of dawn in order to drive into London and obviously my brain isn't properly in gear. OK, what's the punchline?'

'There is no punchline. I'm not joking. I'm deadly serious,' Connor said, his sober expression verifying his words. 'Hell, put an unattached woman and an unattached man in regular proximity and if they're both blessed with a healthy sex drive the chances are that, sooner or later, they'll strike sparks off each other. It's human nature.'

'Is it? I'm not sure I'd go along with that,' she said, feeling harassed all over again. She drew in a breath. 'However—'

'Don't reject the idea out of hand.'

'But—'

'Take your time and consider it.' He placed a white porcelain mug of steaming coffee in front of her and returned to the machine to fill one for himself. 'Weigh up the pros and cons, like I have.' Looking back over his shoulder, he flashed her a crooked grin. 'Humour me. OK?'

Jennet frowned. Her mind might be spinning like a windmill in a hurricane, but he sounded unemotive, matter-of-fact and so damn reasonable. As if he were conducting a business transaction. He also sounded as if he believed she would be persuaded by his sales pitch and fall in line with the idea, in due course. She would not. Yet point-blank objection seemed to be getting her nowhere, so she supposed she might as well go through the motions and *pretend* to consider. Indeed, his insistence left little alternative.

Sighing, she gave a reluctant shrug. 'OK.'

Whilst his announcement had surprised and stunned, this 'sock it to her' approach was typical, she thought as she folded the newspaper and placed it inside the black leather attaché case which stood at her feet. Connor Malone believed in plain speaking and decisive actions. In his role of executive producer, with responsibility for Ensign's entire drama output and director of a few selected programmes, if he wanted something he went for it with a steely determination; and was invariably successful. Her heart pounded. But now he wanted *her*.

Jennet looked at where her suitor lounged with a broad shoulder against the full-length window, drinking his coffee as he gazed down at the forecourt car park which stretched out below and the chairman's designated space which patently remained empty. Clad in a blue cord shirt and faded Levis, he was six feet two inches of well-muscled and athletic proportions.

With thickly lashed grey eyes, dark brown hair which persisted in flopping over his forehead and a chiselled mouth, he must have veered perilously close to choirboy-cute when he was younger, she mused. A pretty boy. But now his features were lean, a vertical line grooved each closely shaven cheek, he had a sprinkling of silver at his temples. Now Connor Malone was handsome.

Jennet swallowed. She supposed she must have always known that he was good-looking—and virile and sexy—yet it had never *hit* her before. Abruptly, it did. Hard. Like a blow beneath the heart. A sharp, craftily angled blow which left her breathless, helpless, disoriented. Wham! All of a sudden he had ceased to fit into the benignly neutral slot of work associate, and had become rawly and disconcertingly *male*.

She gazed at him in bewilderment. Why had she remained immune for so long? How could she have been so blinkered and blithely unaware? All right, she did not spend her days forever on the alert for husky Adonises. Yet neither was she blind. Her immunity seemed strange—though perhaps it could be due to the fact that today was, she realised with a start, the first time they had been alone together.

Since a rush of meetings when her series had been acquired, cast, swiftly put into production, they had met every three to four weeks on average. They had worked together on honing her scripts—Connor suggesting an additional line here, a tightening of pace there—and for her it had been an invaluable learning experience, but whenever they had met there had always been other people around.

People such as secretaries wafting in and out of his office, production assistants sitting in in the hope of picking up tips from the master, or Lester Sewell playing the involved top dog. People who must have obscured the impact of the director's presence. People who had prevented their conversation from becoming personal. But today—today everything had gone haywire.

Jennet gulped down a mouthful of coffee. In the theoretical case of her selecting a candidate for a romantic twosome and marking off required attributes, Connor Malone must score high on any list. In addition to the sex appeal which ensured that whenever he strode through the television centre he left a ripple of feminine sighs in his wake, he was also intelligent, had a finely tuned sense of humour, and possessed the knack of being at ease with himself, without being full of himself. He displayed an admirable dedication towards his work and—

Hang on a minute, she told herself. Don't get carried away. This is theory we're dealing with here, not reality.

The director might be an object of desire in many women's eyes, but not in hers. She felt absolutely no urge to cuddle up close with him. Or with any other man. She enjoyed going solo. Her jaw firmed. She was happy being independent, self-sufficient and in control of her life.

In any case, Connor had a minus marked against him, a galumphing significant damning minus. As well as leaving sighs behind him when he strode, god-like, he also trailed a string of broken hearts. The gossip which seeped into studio conversations like toxic gas had revealed that ever since a dim and distant divorce his love life had taken the form of a succession of dalliances, which he had always ended. Apparently he had not cheated, he had been honest about the limits of his commitment—making it clear that long-term devotion was not his scene—yet his partners had invariably fallen for him and been hurt.

Jennet tucked an errant tendril back into the burnished spice-brown hair which was caught neatly at her nape with a gold barrette. Casanova had staked her out as someone worth conquering, someone who would be yet another notch on his belt? Well, he could forget it.

'I don't want to become involved,' she announced.

Connor swung round from the window. 'Involved?'

'Involved in a love affair with you,' she said, and smiled to soften the rebuff.

She had to work with her would-be romancer now and in the future, so she must not turn him into an enemy. Indeed, he had a critical input into her career, which made it politic to keep everything between them as sweet and light as possible.

'With me?' he said.

Jennet nodded. 'Please don't be offended. I think
you're extremely professional and talented, and I have
a deep respect for your creative judgement. I'm so
grateful you're directing my series because I know it
wouldn't have been half as successful otherwise. A
quarter as successful. I'm very lucky that someone of
your stature agreed to take it on,' she said, and stopped.

In attempting to placate him she had become carried
away again and started to gush—cringingly. Pass the sick
bag, Mary-Lou. She was also straying from the point.
'It's just that I'm not interested in you—erm—' She
shone him another smile. An awkward one. She was
giving the guy the brush-off, after all. 'Like that.'

Connor placed his mug on the tray beside the expresso machine and walked forward, his scuffed sand-
coloured leather boots padding softly over the cord
carpet. He stood beside her, rested a lean hip against
the edge of the table and folded his arms across his chest.

'You're talking about me as a lover?' he said.

Jennet gulped. 'Erm—yes.'

It had been ages since she had discussed anything even
remotely sexual with a man and, whereas he was one
cool cucumber, her poise had begun to fray disastrously
around the edges. She realigned the position of her
notepad and straightened her pen. His closeness disturbed her, too. She had never been bothered by it before,
but now she felt nerve-janglingly aware of his height as
he looked down at her, of his powerful physique, the
inherent masculine energy.

'How do you know you're not interested when you've
never . . . tried me?' A smile hovered around the corners
of his mouth. 'I could be a demon between the sheets.'

One of the reasons why Jennet had been so successful, so quickly as a professional writer was her vivid

imagination—and at his words it shot into overdrive. In her mind's eye she saw Connor naked and in bed with her. He was hard-bodied, smooth-skinned, thrusting. And she was winding her legs around him and whimpering with pleasure.

'I don't know and I shall never know. I don't want to know,' she yammered, frantically banishing the image. 'I'm not in the market for a romance.'

He raked back the fall of dark hair from his brow with blunt-tipped fingers. 'You figure I'm too old for you?' he enquired.

'Too old?' she said, in surprise. 'No. You're—what?'

'Thirty-nine.'

'And I'm thirty-two, so—'

'Thirty-two? I thought you were around twenty-six, twenty-seven.' His gaze flicked over her oval face, the sparkling green eyes, the clear brow, the peach-bloom skin. 'You look amazingly young for your age.'

'It runs in the family,' Jennet said, and her expression momentarily shadowed. 'But an affair doesn't appeal, not with you nor with anyone else. My career has the priority and I'm not prepared to be distracted. Maybe one day the tick of my biological clock will prompt a review—'

'As biological clocks are reputed to do,' he observed drily.

'—but now, and for the foreseeable future, the *status quo* suits me just fine. You won't let this spoil our working relationship, will you?' she carried on. 'Please don't. The last thing I want is for us to—'

'I wasn't suggesting that we should have an affair,' Connor broke in.

She looked up at him. 'No-o?' she said uncertainly.

'No. I was suggesting that two of the characters in *Hutton's Spa* should get it together.'

Silence. A wave of colour swept up her neck to fire her cheeks with scarlet flame. *Hutton's Spa* was the name of her television series.

'Oh,' she said.

CHAPTER TWO

LOWERING her head, Jennet took a hurried gulp of coffee. This had to be the most embarrassing moment of her entire life. Nightmarearoony. If only a giant hand would crash in through the window, snatch her up and carry her away. Far away. To the other side of the earth. Or, better yet, if only Connor could suffer a severe bout of amnesia which would wipe the last ten minutes completely from his mind.

But how could she have made such a naïve and stupid mistake? Why had she jumped in with two feet only to wallow up to her neck in mortification? Because she had been distracted by what she had been reading in the newspaper. Yet their meeting was a story conference to discuss the next run of episodes and future scripts, so she ought to have realised. It was obvious. Screamingly apparent. *Bonehead!* And she should have known that the idea of the director advocating a romance—out of the blue and when he had shown not the merest sign of attraction—was absurd.

Her brain skidded around like a blancmange on ice. Could she talk herself out of this? Was there a way to wriggle free? Suppose she acted the amusing little miss and claimed to have been kidding and 'humouring' him all along? No. It would never work. His credulity would not stretch that far.

'But thanks for considering us joining together in a red-hot liaison. I'm flattered,' Connor continued, and his lips tweaked. 'I hope you're not too disappointed to discover that I wasn't offering what you believed I was offering?'

Her head lifted. Her chin jutted. 'Disappointed? Me? You've heard of a hollow laugh? If I knew how to do one, I would. And how patronising, how condescending, what an arrogant assumption! You may ripple elastic wherever you go, but you are not *that* good-looking,' she said witheringly. 'Your nose has a definite hook and your jaw's too severe. You do not have The World's Most Beautiful Man written in your passport. Disappointed? Not one scrap!'

'There's no need to feel defensive,' he murmured, looking amused by her outburst.

'I don't. I'm not. If you recall, I rejected your offer,' Jennet pointed out, in a desperate attempt to salvage a few shreds of dignity.

'Only after giving it some very, very serious thought,' he drawled.

She glared. She might have been a total Betty Boop, but he had deliberately strung her along and played games. He had had fun at her expense and now looked as if he was on the verge of chuckling fit to bust. How dared he?

'You wouldn't listen to me when I said no, so I *pretended* to think,' she informed him haughtily.

Connor arched a brow. 'Is that correct?'

'Yes, it damn well is! So you can take that smirk off your face.'

'But if you were just faking, why subject me to such an intense scrutiny?'

Her cheeks flamed hot again. She had not realised that he had been aware of her looking at him.

'Because it had struck me how different we are. How unsuited. How you are not my type,' Jennet said, snapping out the words.

Never mind about sweetness and light. She was furious about being tricked, and determined to puncture his ego.

'You mean I'm too laid-back?' Connor asked, sliding his hands into the pockets of his jeans, which stretched the denim tight across his thighs, outlining the bulge of his sex.

She gave a thin smile. 'Something like that.'

His manner, how he wore his clothes, even the ancient Morgan sports car he drove—from beneath the seats of which, so the gossips whispered, could be unearthed hastily discarded items of women's underwear—fell into the laid-back category. The director was carelessly graceful. Relaxed. Or, to be accurate, his manner was relaxed most of the time, she adjusted, recalling his determination. There were occasions when his grey eyes would darken to charcoal, his jaw would clench and he would make his wishes known in no uncertain terms. Then it paid to tread with care.

Yet she liked his laid-back style and found it attractive. His *laissez-faire* held infinite charm. What she did not approve of—where the crucial difference lay between them—was his history of casual conquests. Affairs as affairs were not for her. She valued reliability. And if she should choose to share her life again—*if*—it would be with a family-minded man who could be trusted with permanence and happy-ever-after. Not a 'love 'em and leave 'em' specialist like Connor Malone.

A thought suddenly occurred to her. Whilst his assessment of himself was apt, mightn't it also be interpreted as an assessment of her? Couldn't it be a backhanded criticism?

'Are you implying that I'm too uptight?' Jennet demanded. She shot a downward glance at the navy business suit which she wore with a high-necked cream silk blouse, navy-toned stockings and navy high-heeled shoes. 'Because I spend so much of my time at home writing and slopping around in a sweater and jeans, when I come up to London I like to dress smartly. But if you think that means I'm prim and proper you have totally the wrong impression. Which characters were you thinking might get together?' she asked, in an abrupt veer.

She had been justifying her appearance and defending herself against his apparent charge, but why? There was no need. She had nothing to prove to him. She knew she wasn't prissy and she did not give two beans about his personal opinion of her. What she did care about was their working alliance.

'Beth and Craig,' he replied.

Something nipped inside her. Something crawled. 'Never,' Jennet said, vigorously shaking her head.

Both characters were members of the staff at *Hutton's Spa*, which was a country mansion health farm owned by Dinsdale Hutton, an affable aristocratic layabout, and his business-brain wife, Madeleine. Beth, who, like Dinsdale, was in her late forties, worked there as a masseuse, while Craig was a strapping young gardener.

'Why not?' Connor protested. 'OK, Beth's around twenty years his senior, but women do have toyboys.'

'I'm well aware of that,' she said, and heard herself speak sharply. Too sharply. Pushing back her chair, Jennet walked over to the expresso machine and placed her empty mug on the tray. 'An affair between Beth and Craig would be . . . icky.'

'Icky?'

'Hackneyed,' she redefined.

'I disagree. I believe it would add a fizz to the proceedings so, as I said before, please give it your consideration. *Please,*' he repeated, when she started to object—though the word could be recognised as an instruction rather than a request. 'You must've thought that "I reckon it's time we began a love affair" was one heck of an opening gambit,' Connor remarked, strolling up to where she stood.

She pinned on a smile. Whatever he said, however close he came, this time she would remain cool, calm and collected. He would not be allowed to ruffle her composure.

'It did seem a tad blunt, even for you,' she replied lightly. 'Especially when we hadn't held hands. Or whispered sweet nothings.'

'Or kissed,' he added, and paused, his gaze falling to her full mouth. 'Perhaps we should remedy that?'

Jennet kept her smile resolutely in place. His expression might have become grave, but he was playing with her, again. The louse. However, she would show him that two could play games and, in the process, demonstrate that he did not have a monopoly on being laid-back.

'Why not?' she said, and, raising her face to his, she puckered up her lips.

As Connor looked down at her, she saw the surprise flicker in the depths of his eyes. He did not move. Gotcha! she thought triumphantly. The biter is bit. She was congratulating herself on having so satisfyingly called his bluff when he stepped forward and bent his dark head.

The touch of his lips on hers sent the blood chasing through her veins. It made her heart pump. It dizzied her mind. She had not expected him to meet her challenge, but she refused to do what *he* would expect and pull back. Jennet gazed steadily into the grey eyes which were so close to hers. OK, she had the grim-set squint of someone having their eyes tested, but she would not be flustered. It was just a kiss and she had been kissed before. Lots of times.

When his arm came around her waist and he gathered her to him, she did not protest. A protest was what he wanted. She felt the hardness of his body against hers, smelled his clean fresh smell. She was thinking that she could understand why women—other women, silly women—went into ecstasies about him when his tongue thrust silkily between her lips.

She stiffened—wasn't this going too far?—but as she tasted him her senses leapt. This was not 'just a kiss'. It was a kiss which excited and aroused, which made her eyelids fall. Which made her want more.

Sliding a hand up over his shoulder, Jennet curled it around his neck. All thought of withdrawal had gone. All coherent thought had vanished. She strained closer. The kiss deepened and lengthened, tongues twisted and moistly twined, until finally they were forced to come up for air.

'Wow,' Connor said softly. He inhaled a breath. 'For someone who reckons she'd need to be dragged kicking and screaming into an affair you—'

'It's been a long time since—since anyone kissed me—erm, like that,' she yattered, taking a jerky backward step and putting some much needed space between them.

Why had she entered so willingly into the embrace? she wondered. Why had she allowed it to go on, and on, and blissfully on? She did not know, but she needed to give him a reason and attempt an excuse.

'You and me both,' he said.

'You?' Jennet protested, in transparent disbelief.

A muscle tightened in his jaw. 'If I'd been as rampant as rumour central here apparently suggests, my vital organs would've been pickled long ago, placed in a jar and be the star attraction at some museum of biological marvels,' he said drolly. Turning, he strode towards the door. 'Perhaps Lester's forgotten about our meeting.'

'Lester?' It took her a moment to manage the necessary mental leap. 'Oh—yes.'

'He's usually on time and he'd have rung in if he'd been delayed, so I'll go and have a word with his secretary to see if she can throw any light.'

'Erm—good idea.'

As the door clicked shut behind him, Jennet sank down onto her chair. She felt weak at the knees. What had happened to her common sense? To misinterpret his talk of a love affair had been bad enough, but to invite him to kiss her and proceed to join in had been crazy. Bizarre. Never mind her knees, she had gone weak in the head.

The only relief—a huge relief—was that Connor would not be drawing her into a clinch again. He might have masked it well, but the dazed look in his eyes when the embrace had ended had said he had been as taken aback by its spiralling heat as she. Yet the daze had almost instantly been replaced by wariness then, just as quickly, by annoyance. And his speedy exit could be recognised as an escape.

He had desired her—fleetingly—and regretted it. There would be no repeat performance. Jennet gave a wry smile. From now on, he would keep her strictly at arm's length, which, whilst it could be construed as uncomplimentary, was where she wanted to be.

She flipped open the cover of her folder. The kiss was over and done with. An inexplicable unfortunate blip. She would erase it from her memory and had no doubt that Connor would do the same—if he had not done so already. They had returned to their comfortably neutral working relationship. Her brow crinkled. More or less.

She took out the topmost sheet of paper. Much time had been spent thinking up plotlines for the next series, developing them into treatments, and writing the first episode in full. She had summarised everything in one page of notes and she read through them again. Whether comic or dramatic, the plotlines were strong, but they did not include a love affair. Her chin tilted in defiance. She saw no need for a toyboy love affair. None.

Jennet waited, drumming her fingers in a restless staccato on the edge of the table. When Connor failed to reappear and her thoughts started sneaking traitorously back to their kiss, she reached down again for the newspaper. It was a copy of last week's *Barton Chronicle*, a small circulation journal which covered life in the sleepy Devonshire town of Barton Crouch and surrounding villages.

She had lived in Barton Crouch during her early teens and the paper had been sent by Mrs Henson, who had worked in the house as daily help and part-time baby-sitter. She and the now elderly lady had formed an affectionate bond and despite the passing of the years and her changes of address they still kept in touch, though these days it was usually through the exchange of birthday and Christmas cards.

Leafing through, she found the article. 'Thought you might be interested,' Mrs Henson had written across the top of the page in her spidery scrawl. 'P.S. Don't worry, I shan't blab.'

STILL A BEAUTY AT FIFTY PLUS, a headline announced above a photograph of an elegant, smiling woman whose delicate features, unlined skin and slim figure confirmed the claim. Clad in a bare-armed dress with a long, wrap-around skirt and curled up kittenishly in the corner of a sofa, she looked as if she had barely struggled into her forties.

The article explained how the woman, Tina Lemoine, who had once owned a house in the area, had returned for a brief visit and reluctantly agreed to be interviewed. Jennet raised amused brows. Reluctantly?

Most of the facts were a recapping mishmash of how, back in the early sixties, Tina had dabbled in modelling, gained fame as the sought-after and fought-over girl-friend of rock musicians, and could lay claim to being one of the original 'swingers'. The article sympathised about her never finding 'any man who could replace my wonderful first husband', skated over the haphazard love life she had enjoyed ever since and said that the 'delightful divorcee' was currently living in a flower-filled villa on Portugal's Algarve coast. The fawning tone made it clear the male reporter had been bewitched by his interviewee. Surprise, surprise, she thought wryly.

But what was a surprise, and an unpleasant one, was the final paragraph.

Although Tina has a daughter, Jay, by her first marriage to the long-deceased barrister Michael Brinsley, she refused to say anything about her only child, apart from the tantalising comment that she was 'making a name for herself'. How is the young lady making her name? we wonder. Where is she now? Perhaps one of our readers knows? If so, please get in touch and help us to trace her.

Jennet frowned. She was Tina Lemoine's daughter, always called Jay as a child. She had inherited her mother's fine bone structure and cat-like green eyes, but her hair was mid-brown and not clouds of give-away silvery blonde. Thank goodness. When she was younger she had been open about the relationship, but these days she preferred to keep it a secret. Keeping quiet allowed her to escape the hullabaloo which having a celebrity parent invariably and tiresomely inspired.

Her mother's delight in her writing prowess meant she would have spoken about her without thinking, she reflected as she put the newspaper away. But why must the Press be so inquisitive and intrusive? She did not want to be tracked down, 'outed' and featured in their columns. Tina might bask in the limelight which had followed her in sporadic bursts from the sixties, but privacy mattered to her.

Jennet bit deep into the cushiony fullness of her lower lip. It mattered because she preferred to live quietly and without fuss, but also because with publicity could come a danger that—

The thought was sliced off. She would not be traced. Mrs Henson had promised to keep quiet and who else in Barton Crouch knew of her whereabouts? No one. The letters which had flowed between her and schoolgirl friends when she had first left the town had dried up years ago, so if any of those friends still lived there and should chance upon the article they would be unable to make chase. She had no need to worry.

'Lester's secretary reminded him of our meeting as he was leaving yesterday and doubts he's forgotten, but she hasn't a clue where he is,' Connor reported, walking back into the office. 'She tried to call him on his mobile, but no luck. Then I went along to check with the traffic desk.

Seems there's a major snarl-up on the M4, which is his route in, so it looks like he could be trapped there.'

Jennet grimaced. Motorway jams could take forever to clear. 'Oh, hell.'

'My sentiments exactly.'

'Can't we start without him?' she appealed. 'Let's be honest, Lester's going to agree to whatever you say.'

He rubbed pensive fingers along the edge of his jaw. 'Better not. We'd better observe protocol. He is the boss.'

Lester Sewell might be the boss and wish to be seen as the boss, yet he always deferred to Connor. With good reason, she thought. A flamboyant, hard-headed businessman from the tough streets of London's East End, Lester had recognised the money to be made from creating and marketing quality programmes, but it was the executive producer who guaranteed that quality. In his five years with Ensign, Connor had been instrumental in garnering a clutch of awards. These had given the company a much envied prestige within the industry, meant soaring profits and had put the chairman forever in his debt.

'Could you come in if we rearrange the meeting for tomorrow?' Connor enquired. 'Same time.'

Jennet heaved a sigh. 'Yes, but the drive from home takes two hours, so I'd rather hang on and hope that Lester turns up soon.'

'It'll need to be pretty soon,' he said, frowning at the heavy stainless-steel watch which was strapped to his broad wrist. 'I have a viewing which I can't miss in a quarter of an hour.'

'Then suppose I tell you the plotlines which I have in mind? You could think about them and—' She broke off as the office door opened and a short, chunky, balding man in his fifties burst in. His bulbous nose reddened by the cold February wind, he wore a natty black woollen overcoat with a velvet collar and carried two large parchment-paper carrier bags. 'Lester!' she said thankfully.

'How's my favourite girl?' he asked, stooping to kiss her cheek. He patted the director's arm. 'Morning, Con. My sincere apologies for keeping you guys waiting,' he went on, dumping the bags on the table and rapidly shedding his coat to reveal a pale blue sharkskin suit. 'Been trying constantly to get in touch, but my cellular's gone wonky.'

'You were stuck on the motorway?' Connor enquired.

'No, I've been shopping.' Diving into a carrier bag, he produced two luxuriously gift-wrapped and satin-bowed boxes. He presented one to Jennet and handed the other to Connor. 'Open up. Thought I'd be in and out of the shop in ten mins max, but the engraving took for ever. Then when I got back to the Jag what did I find but a traffic warden about to book me.' Lester rolled his eyes at the capriciousness of authority. 'Managed to sweet-talk her out of it, though it took some time. Spun her a tale about—'

He was deep into explaining how he had persuaded the woman not to issue a ticket when he realised they were on the point of lifting the lids on their boxes. 'These are a personal token of my thanks to you, my Dream Team. Plus the champagne,' he said, showing them four gold-foil-necked magnums which rested inside the second bag. 'Last night I received the ratings for the final episode of *Hutton's Spa* and—drum roll, drum roll, bring on the dancing girls—' Lester executed a swift soft-shoe shuffle '—it was seen by seven point one million viewers.'

Jennet's jaw dropped and she gaped. 'Seven million?'

The audience had increased with each of the six episodes, but this figure put the show firmly into the 'most popular' bracket. It was success beyond her wildest dreams.

'That's tremendous,' Connor said, and they laughed in delight and grinned at each other like idiots.

'It's brilliant,' the chairman declared exuberantly. 'Con'll be grabbing himself yet another "great directing" trophy and you're going to walk off with this year's Best Writer Award, no question.'

'You think so?' she asked, her eyes swinging to Connor.

'It's been a good year for drama, but I'd say you have an odds-on chance of reaching the shortlist,' he told her, his reply more reasoned than their overlord's claim.

She glowed with pleasure.

'This is brilliant, too,' she said, removing a snowstorm of white tissue paper and lifting out her gift. It was a piece of handmade lead crystal, standing about six inches tall and etched with the lifelike figure of an upright, twig-carrying beaver. Discreetly engraved on a rock beside the animal was the name of the programme, the viewing figure and date. She reached up to kiss her benefactor's cheek. 'Thank you very much.'

'And many thanks from me,' Connor said, holding aloft a graceful lead crystal tiger which was reared up on its hind legs and looked ready to spring. 'It's superb.'

Lester grinned. 'Pleased you like 'em. Thought they were in character.'

'Me being the eager beaver?' Jennet asked, with a smile.

'Dead right, and Connor being a tiger for keeping everyone up to scratch and maintaining high standards.' The chairman commented on the wonderful viewing

figure again and repeated his thanks. There were more
mutual expressions of delight. 'Now to business,' he declared, taking his place at the head of the table. 'Con?'

'Whilst an audience of seven million is excellent, it
doesn't mean we can afford to be complacent,' the director said, walking around the table to draw out a high-
backed chair and sit down opposite her. 'With the second
series, we must make sure we retain our existing viewers
and increase the numbers.' He slung her a look. 'We do
that with stories which grab and hold.'

'And the stories I suggest are...' Lifting her summary,
Jennet read through it and then took the papers from
her folder. 'This is the script for the first episode,' she
said, handing a copy to each man. 'I'll explain the general
gist.'

'You've been burning the midnight oil,' Lester remarked a few minutes later when she paused to turn a
page.

She smiled. 'I've worked every day for the last two
months.'

'Including weekends?' he protested, and she nodded.
'No time off to go gallivanting with a boyfriend?'

'No boyfriend,' she replied, and continued relating the
storyline.

How come a lovely young woman like Jennet
Galbraith didn't have a man in her life? Connor wondered as he listened. Lester had told him how it was three
years since her husband had died and after three years
she could be expected to be seeing someone again. After
three years, it seemed reasonable for her to have
remarried.

Jennet *was* lovely, though it had never truly registered
with him before. With expressive green eyes fringed by
sooty black lashes, high cheekbones elbowing their way

out and that tantalisingly full mouth, she was a striking-looking girl. His gaze dipped to the pout of her breasts in the no-nonsense business suit and lower to the slimness of her waist. She also had a delectable shape.

He frowned. He had been aware of her as smart, pleasant and lively, someone with whom he worked easily—yet he had never thought about her as an alluring woman. A seriously fanciable woman. Why not? He cast around in his mind for a reason, and decided that it must have been because she had kept their relationship strictly business and never given out any sexual vibes. Because she had resolutely failed to acknowledge the fact that she was female and he was male...until today.

Connor cursed silently. Kissing her had been an error. Whilst, being a red-blooded male, he had had his share of romances, he had always retained a moral dimension. He did not become involved with married women. He acted responsibly sex-wise. He steered clear of workplace affairs, which could only cause trouble. Today he had foolishly and unaccountably broken the third golden rule. Never again.

'Comments?' Jennet asked, reaching the end of her explanations and looking up.

'It all sounds like super stuff to me,' Lester declared robustly.

'I'm happy to go with the first episode and, in general, with your other ideas, apart from the fire in the gymnasium,' Connor said. 'A fire on that scale would be expensive to stage.'

The chairman nodded in prompt agreement. 'Too expensive.'

'I could make the fire smaller,' she suggested.

'You could also drop it altogether and write a love affair between Beth and Craig,' Connor stated, his eyes meeting hers.

'But I don't—' she began earnestly.

'It has my vote,' Lester proclaimed. 'A spot of rumpy-pumpy always pleases the punters and, come to think of it, *Hutton's Spa* hasn't had any yet. Yes, that's what we need.'

'Sorry, I have to go now,' Connor said, inspecting his watch and getting to his feet. 'I'm assessing the pilot of a possible sit-com and everyone'll be waiting for me.'

'I have to make a move too,' the older man said. He went to reclaim his coat and pulled it on. 'What I suggest is that you write the episodes as you've described,' he carried on, smiling at Jennet, 'but leave out the fire. Connor has a firm handle on what appeals and some heavy breathing between Beth and Craig sounds terrific to me.'

'I don't—' she tried again, but he held up a silencing hand.

'No need to make a decision now. The episode's one of the later ones, so we can discuss it again at a later date. You were talking about going down to Sussex for a day or two of filming while there's a chance in April,' he said, turning to Connor.

'Yes, given decent weather.'

The chairman looked at her. 'How's about we have a pow-wow then? You live close by and it'll save you having to come up to London.'

'That'd be good,' she replied.

'If I remember right, you haven't managed to get to any outside filming before?'

'No, on the previous occasions I was abroad.'

'Then you'll be able to see what happens. My secretary'll ring you with the date nearer the time. Apologies again for being late and for making this such a brief meeting, though we've covered everything.' Going to the door, Lester raised a hand in farewell. 'Take care,' he said, and disappeared.

Jennet gathered up her papers, pushed them into the folder and rammed it into the attaché case. 'Thanks. Thanks a bundle,' she said, scowling at Connor as she snapped shut the locks. She all but stamped her foot in annoyance. 'You knew you'd get Lester on your side.'

'It's not a question of taking sides,' he replied calmly. 'It's a question of what'll draw in the viewers and—'

'Having Beth and Craig canoodle doesn't interest me and if it doesn't interest me I won't be able to write it effectively,' she declared, her green eyes glittering. 'Sorry, it's no go.'

'Would you care to run that past me again?' he said, in a low voice which carried a warning thread of steel.

Her chin lifted. She refused to be warned off. She would not be intimidated. 'It is no go,' she pronounced, separating the words and firing them at him like bullets.

'Have you been having assertiveness training from Attila the Hun?' he enquired.

'If I'm taking a more assertive stance it's because I object to being railroaded,' she responded, putting two bottles of champagne into the empty bag.

'This is not railroading,' he said impatiently. 'All I'm asking is that you don't trash the idea outright, but allow it to marinate for at least five minutes.'

'It has marinated for five minutes and it stinks!' She thrust the bag at him across the table. 'These are yours.'

He ignored the champagne. 'You've always agreed to any changes which I've suggested in the past. You've always co-operated.'

'So?'

'So why join the awkward squad all of a sudden? Is it the prospect of having to write sex scenes which is worrying you?' Connor asked abruptly. 'Don't let it. When I spoke of joyous abandon and free-floating lust, I was exaggerating. And the programme's watched by families so the sex can't be too explicit. All we need is—'

'Sex scenes don't bother me,' she cut in. 'I'm perfectly capable of writing them, if required. Writing them with realism, with tingle and building up a good head of steam. I'm not frigid.'

His eyes met hers. 'I believe you,' he said.

A blush crept into her skin. It had been the idea that he might consider her prim and proper which had prompted the impetuous declaration, but she knew he was thinking about their kiss.

'However, I shall not be writing about Beth with Craig,' she completed.

His lips tightened. 'I never realised you could be so goddamn stubborn!'

'You learn something new every day,' she said pertly. 'That's what makes life interesting.'

'Why are you hostile towards a toyboy affair?' Connor demanded. He fixed her with a piercing gaze. 'Is there some special reason?'

She became busy, swaddling the crystal beaver in tissue paper again and putting it back into the box. 'I simply think that it seems predictable.'

'Which makes it a natural progression.'

'In your opinion, but not mine.' Jennet picked up the carrier bag in one hand and her attaché case in the other. 'I may be a newcomer to television and you may be a big shot, but that doesn't mean you are always right,' she said, and, with her head held high, she stalked past him and out of the room.

CHAPTER THREE

JENNET placed her foot on the rough-hewn step of the wooden stile, swung herself up and sat astride it. Hugging the folder which she carried to her, she looked back across the valley. She smiled. It was heaven on earth in the April sunshine. The woods she had walked down through had been carpeted in violet bluebells, new-born lambs frolicked and baa-ed in the fields, fresh spring green leaves shimmered on budding trees.

Her gaze travelled in a forward arc. Ahead, beyond the vast stretch of playing fields, a mansion rose up against the clear blue sky. It was Hammingden School. During term-time over two hundred boys jostled in the corridors, studied at desks, played sports, some as weekly boarders, others as day pupils. But it was the Easter holidays. The boys had scattered, the school was closed and a distant cluster of tiny indiscernible figures indicated that a film shoot was in progress.

Lester, who had contacts in the most surprising places, was friendly with the headmaster, had once called on him at the school and, some years later, had remembered it as a suitable—and economical—*Hutton's Spa*. He had brought Connor to view it, received his approval, and a mutually satisfactory deal had been done.

Jennet eyed the Victorian brick building. With a central archway, ivy-clad twin towers and stained-glass windows, it was impressive. Her opinion had not been sought in the choice, but when Lester had arranged for the headmaster to show her around she had agreed that,

34

having spacious grounds, tennis courts and a swimming pool, the school made an attractive and credible health farm. Her mouth curved. So credible that some viewers had written in asking for a brochure!

Swinging over a denimmed leg, she jumped down from the stile. It was early afternoon and she was on her way to watch an hour or two of filming before taking part in the pow-wow which had been fixed back in February.

Back then she had been wondering whether her identity as her mother's daughter might be revealed for public consumption, she recalled as she started off across the playing fields. There had been no need to fret. The response to the *Barton Chronicle's* quest had been zero, as anticipated. The reporter had repeated his appeal for two subsequent weeks, but then, so Mrs Henson had reported when she'd rung Jennet, had acknowledged the pointlessness and dropped it. Her mother had also been reminded of Jennet's request that she did not, repeat not, talk about her to journalists.

'Forgive me, darling,' Tina had said, in her husky voice. 'I'm so proud of you, it just slipped out. Personally I don't see that one comment is such a big deal or that a spot of publicity would go amiss, but if you insist I shall keep mousey quiet in future.'

Jennet grinned. She felt like punching the air and belting out a chorus of 'Zip A Dee Do Dah,' but satisfied herself instead with an impromptu hoppity-skip. One worry had vanished and—she glanced at the mêlée of distant figures—so had another. She performed a second hoppity-skip.

Abruptly she halted, put her folder down on the grass and drew her orange-red cotton-knit sweater off over her head. Stretching both arms out wide, she flapped them up and down. Phew! That felt better. Walking in

the sunshine was hot work. She pulled her white T-shirt
out of the waistband of her jeans and tucked it in again,
tighter. Knotting the arms of the sweater loosely around
her shoulders, she smoothed back her mane of silky
brown hair and retrieved the folder.

Her trek was resumed—and her thoughts. Although,
over the past six weeks, she had spoken to Connor several
times on the phone and he had sent faxes asking her to
do some rewriting which would add more dramatic
thrust, he had not mentioned the Beth/Craig union
again. Male pride might have stopped him from ac-
knowledging her better judgement—which was a shame;
she would've enjoyed hearing him grovel—but his silence
meant he had ditched the idea. Praise be. And an hour
ago, via word processor and ink-jet, she had printed out
the last page of an alternative episode. She hoppity-
skipped again. It was a cracker of an episode.

'Hey!' a voice shouted, breaking into her reverie.

Her head jerked up and Jennet saw that as she was
cutting diagonally across the top corner of the playing
fields, Connor had set off from the school and was
walking straight towards her. He wore a grey sweatshirt
with black jeans and his hair fell in dark spikes over his
brow. He looked lithe and graceful and athletic.

Her footsteps faltered and stopped. She had told
herself that when she saw him again she would discover
he was ordinary and that her image of him as knuckle-
gnawingly desirable had been a silly moment of over-
heated imagination. Yet already she knew it was not so.
Even with him twenty or thirty yards away, her heart
had started to clatter behind her ribcage. How juvenile!
How irritating!

Standing straighter, Jennet gave herself a stern 'get a
grip!' lecture. She was not some man-worshipping bimbo

with a tendency to drool, she was an intelligent and independent woman. As she watched Connor approach, it registered that the crew behind him had been put on hold. Also that his stride was purposeful and his expression determined. A smile bubbled up inside her. The director had abandoned filming in order to come and speak to her—the writer.

She had read of how, when stage or film dialogue was suddenly discovered to be too lengthy or too brief, the writer would be consulted. He or she would then dash off a few pertinent jewelled phrases which would resolve the impasse, allow production to continue and be showered with gratitude. By the mega ton.

This had not happened to her. On the occasions when she had visited the studios, the dialogue had needed no adjustment and, in truth, she had felt little more than a bystander. The bubbling smile swelled. But this was her moment of glory. She had arrived in the nick of time, at the crucial instant of need, to the rescue.

'Where do you think you're going?' Connor demanded, striding up to her.

Jennet looked at him. She had imagined a relieved 'thank heavens you're here to save us all' kind of greeting, but instead he sounded brusque. Though he would be worried, she reasoned. Time was of the essence and delays cost money. His informal style belied a sharp business sense and the keen eye which he kept on budgets was something else which had earned him the esteem of Ensign's chairman.

'I was intending to join Diana,' she explained, gesturing across to where white plastic tables and chairs had been arranged on the lawn to one side of the main school building.

At them waited actors whose services were not presently required. Some chatted, others learned their lines, and amongst them sat a Titian-haired woman in her early forties, looking through a newspaper. She was Diana Gower, who played the part of the business-brain wife. When Jennet had gone, nervously and a little shyly, to watch the filming of the very first episode of *Hutton's Spa*, the actress had been quick to welcome her and they had struck up a friendship.

'So you make a beeline for her?' Connor enquired.

'Yes.' Close up, his expression did not seem so much determined as angry. And his stance reminded her of the glass tiger—fierce, poised and ready to spring. Ready to spring on its prey and rip it to shreds. 'Why not?' she asked.

'Because we're bloody filming, that's why not!' he exploded. 'We were in the middle of a take when who bunny-hops into the background, strips off her sweater and makes like a crazed albatross preparing for lift-off?' He jabbed a furious finger at her. 'You!'

'The camera picked me up?' Jennet protested.

'In glorious Technicolor.'

She looked at him in confusion. 'I had no idea,' she began, but he was not listening.

'Then, after the albatross fandango has been safely captured on celluloid, you continue undressing. Out comes the T-shirt from your pants and, for a moment, it seems like you might strip that off, too.' His eyes dipped to the curves of her breasts. 'If you had and we'd screened it, everyone would've forgotten about the actors and focused on you. Though doubtless viewing figures would've soared,' he remarked astringently, 'so who am I to complain?'

She flushed. It was squirm-inducing enough to know that her somewhat kooky progress had been monitored, but also the unit were watching and waiting, and now every single one of the actors at the tables had turned their way. They were the focus of all eyes. Her fingers curled into fists. She did not appreciate being bawled out so roundly and so publicly.

'I'm sorry if I've ruined the take. I apologise,' she said, her voice tart. 'Though it was unintentional. As you know, I don't have any experience of outside filming and I didn't realise I was in the line of the camera, nor that I could be seen at such a distance. However, I shall be far more alert in future.'

'See that you are. See that you don't wreck everything again,' he rasped, and swivelled and marched back to the film unit.

Jennet glowered at his tall, retreating figure. The tiger had pounced—on her, she thought resentfully, and stomped away towards the tables.

'You were getting your wrist smacked?' Diana said sympathetically as she flung herself down in a chair beside her.

'My bottom thrashed, more like, and for the world to see.'

'Never mind, sweetie. Happens to us all from time to time.'

'Maybe, but—' She scowled. 'Connor Malone is definitely *not* my type!'

A plucked brow slanted. 'You like short fat ugly guys?'

'Love them,' she vowed, and looked around. 'Speaking of which, have you seen Lester?'

'No. I heard the Numero Uno was to honour us with his presence, but he hasn't turned up as yet.'

'Oh, well, at least he didn't witness me being slated. How's everything been going?' Jennet asked, indicating the shoot which had started again beneath the arch and damping down on her annoyance. Connor might make her want to jump up and down in a fury, but it was unfair to be tetchy with others. 'I did intend to come along yesterday and then this morning, but—'

'You thought that now you know filming isn't the glamorous activity which you once imagined but consists mainly of waiting around, you'd give it a miss?' the actress enquired.

She grinned. After only a couple of visits to the set she had become bored and decided to space her attendance.

'You have a point, but the fact is that I was finishing a script.'

'Everything's been going well,' Diana said, belatedly answering her question. 'The weather's tailor-made.' Peering at the sky, she grimaced. 'So far, but I notice that one or two nasty little clouds are starting to creep in. Uh-uh, seems like Henry's fouled up.'

Connor had halted the action and was speaking to Henry Rawden, the actor who, being lazy, louche and a professional charmer, was ideally cast in the role of Dinsdale. Connor would be asking for some gesture or inflection which *he* wanted and Henry would agree. Of course, Jennet thought drily. When she had been at the studios, she had noticed how everyone—whether it be cast, cameraman, wardrobe mistress or props—seemed to spontaneously obey his demands. She eyed the folder which she had placed on the table. Everyone except her.

But, leaving any personal resistance aside, why should she snap to attention, salute and say 'Yes, sir. No, sir. Three bags full, sir'? Defiance sparked in her green eyes.

The director might have years of experience, but the characters were *her* characters, *her* creations. She decided what they should or should not do, and she saw no reason to make them jump through hoops to oblige him.

Her gaze returned to Connor, who had signalled for the take to resume and was standing beside the camera. His long legs were set apart, his gaze was keen, he oozed concentration. She tugged fractiously at the knotted sleeves of her sweater.

Over the past six weeks she had spent a lot of time thinking about him. Too much time. She never used to think about him, but her revised perception of the man and their kiss had changed everything. Now, at unguarded moments—and often when she was in bed—he would steal into her mind. Dangerously. Thrillingly.

No more, Jennet resolved. Not after today. She refused to entertain flights of fantasy—and unwelcome ones—about someone who had marched up and torn strips off her for what had been an entirely understandable mistake. She refused to waste time on— A sigh emerged. Who was she kidding? She had itched to administer a punch which would have knocked her accuser flat on his back, and, whilst that would have been no easy task, knocking him out of her mind would be even harder.

'I thought you reckoned Connor didn't appeal?' Diana said, with a teasing smile.

'He doesn't,' she replied, realising that she had been staring at him. For how long? Five minutes . . . or ten? It must have been an appreciable length of time, because the take had moved on to another. 'I was—erm—just intrigued by how well Henry fleshes out Dinsdale's character. Anything interesting in *The Comet*?' she carried on, eager to change the subject. 'Because I've been working flat out, I haven't looked at a paper in days.'

'Not a thing,' the older woman said, picking up the tabloid which she had been reading. 'One of the technicians'd jettisoned it and I grabbed it, but frankly it's not my cup of tea. No, wait,' she said suddenly, 'I tell a lie. There's a bit about Tina Lemoine. Don't know why, but I always find her fascinating.'

Jennet instinctively stiffened. 'Tina Lemoine?' she repeated.

Media mentions of her mother tended to be intermittent, separated by many months and sometimes by years. It was unusual for another to crop up so quickly, especially as 'the delightful divorcee' had returned to Portugal and, so she had laughingly lamented, not been interviewed again.

'She's way before your time and I dare say her name doesn't ring too many bells, but although she never actually *did* anything much Tina was quite the little star in the early sixties. The woman was appallingly beautiful and still is. It ain't fair,' Diana complained, reaching the gossip-column page. 'There's a picture of her. See?'

When she leant over, Jennet recognised the photograph. It had been taken a couple of years ago, when her mother had attended the launch of a record album made by The Sloop, a male menopausal pop group, one member of which was an ex-lover. The album had been designed to rake in fresh wealth to fill dwindling coffers, but despite much florid hype it had sunk without trace.

'What does the column say?' she asked.

'Seems the reporter happened across some little backwoods paper which was trying to locate Tina's daughter.

They didn't have any luck, so now he's decided to take up the challenge.'

Jennet went hot and cold. Her stomach churned. *The Comet* was a national daily newspaper, read by millions.

'Oh, Lord!' she muttered.

'A rotter, isn't he? No thought that the poor girl might prefer to remain incognito. Just hoping to stimulate reader interest by running a campaign.'

'Diana, you're on,' a girl with a clipboard shouted.

'Coming. This should be the last take and just as well,' the actress remarked, looking at a bank of dark clouds which had filled the horizon and were edging steadily closer. 'The light's going.'

As her companion departed, Jennet picked up the newspaper and feverishly read the column. The reporter repeated the quote about Tina saying how her daughter was 'making a name for herself', declared himself intrigued, and explained that although he had tried to get in touch with Tina in the hope of persuading her to divulge more he had been unsuccessful. So would anyone who knew the daughter—or perhaps even Tina Lemoine's daughter herself—please ring his desk at *The Comet*?

Jennet sat rigid. The chances of her being identified by this appeal were vastly greater than those of her being identified through the *Barton Chronicle*. If she should be named and photographed—heaven forbid!—millions of people would see the picture. Amongst them there might be one person—a stranger who had rushed to give assistance on a dark night—who could recognise her, recall the argument which he must have overheard, put two and two together and make four. Icy talons clawed along her spine. A sleazy, shaming, soul-destroying four.

Thinking furiously, Jennet stared down. *The Comet* was one of the tackier down-market tabloids which featured short, sensational sentences cobbled around pictures of pneumatic-bosomed pin-ups, so the millions who read it were unlikely to include anyone who might be able and willing to identify her. She hoped. She prayed. Though people could pick the paper up by chance, like Diana. But they would not read it in such time-killing detail and the appeal was tucked away at the foot of the page.

So how real was the threat of exposure? She was trying to convince herself that it must be small when she became aware of activity around her. She looked up. Everyone was gathering together their belongings and leaving the tables.

'It's raining,' an actor said as he sped past her.

Picking up her folder, Jennet rose to her feet. The leaden clouds hung overhead and it had started to drizzle. This was causing a general surge towards the archway, where, she saw, filming had come to a stop. As she belatedly followed the hurrying figures, the girl with the clipboard bellowed out.

'That's a wrap. All finished. Home time, folks,' she called.

At her announcement, white-coated assistants scuttled out from a catering wagon which was parked at the side of the school and began to carry away the tables and chairs. Cameras were whisked into enormous aluminium boxes and serpentine cables coiled up. Actors scurried off through the veil of rain to change in the pantechnicon which did duty as dressing rooms. Connor—her gaze seemed to be on a leash and was repeatedly drawn back to him—gave instructions, issued reminders and oversaw.

'Lester hasn't shown up yet?' Diana asked, appearing as she sheltered at the side of the arch.

'No, though I'm still hoping.'

'Must dash, but I'll see you next time you're at the studios.'

Jennet nodded and hugged her. 'Look forward to it. Bye.'

She was wryly watching the speeded-up motion of the people moving back and forth around her, the trucks being loaded, when a telephone shrilled somewhere amongst the crew.

'For you,' called a pony-tailed young man whom she recognised as a production aide, and she saw him handing a mobile phone to Connor.

He answered, exchanged a few sentences and returned the mobile. Looking around, he spotted her and made his way through the dwindling crowd.

'That was Lester,' he announced.

She waited for him to continue, but he didn't. Instead he slid his hands into the hip pockets of his jeans and stood still and silent, frowning at her. Her heart sank. Was he about to embark on a second tongue-lashing? A follow-up condemnation? She straightened her shoulders. This time she would show him—and any audience—that she was no slouch when it came to standing up for herself.

'You look different,' he muttered.

Jennet glanced down. He had not seen her in T-shirt and denims before, nor with her long brown hair swinging loose around her shoulders.

'Not as prim and proper?' she said coolly.

'Right.' Connor roused himself. 'That was Lester calling with the news that today he has been stuck in traffic, on the M25, but he's managed to reach an exit and turn off towards London.'

'So he's not coming here?'

'No. He sends his apologies, but he doesn't have enough time. It seems that it's his thirty-fifth wedding anniversary and he's taking his wife out to dinner at a favourite French restaurant where he's laid on candle-light, violins and a special heart-shaped cake.'

Jennet smiled. She had a sentimental streak a mile wide. 'Nice,' she said. 'I once bumped into the two of them at Heathrow and although it was a hello-and-goodbye because we were catching different flights their affection for each other shone out.'

'They're very close,' he agreed, 'and how great to be happily married for all those years.'

'Wonderful,' she said, and shot him a glance. Connor's tone had sounded wistful, yet it surprised her that someone who had divorced years ago and avoided serious relationships ever since should be extolling matrimony.

'Lester wants us to go ahead without him,' he continued, 'and says he'll rubber-stamp whatever we decide.' He turned to grin at an elderly man in a grey uniform and peaked cap who had ambled up beside them. 'Hi. Joe, isn't it?'

The man nodded and smiled, pleased that he should have remembered. 'Joe the janitor. Is it all right if I lock up the school?' he asked. 'My daughter's invited me over to have my tea with the grandkids and, as you've finished, I'd like to be off.'

'Carry on,' Connor said, and the janitor thanked him and went away.

He might have bawled her out, Jennet thought tartly, but he enjoyed an easy camaraderie with everyone else.

'We were going to talk here, but do you know of a local pub where we could go?' he enquired. 'It's a quiet time of day, so we shouldn't be disturbed. If you'd like to lead the way in your car, I'll follow.'

'I didn't come by car. I walked across the valley and over the playing fields.' She flashed a saccharine smile. 'Remember?'

'With clarity, now that you've reminded me,' he said, his voice clipped. 'So you'll be needing a lift home?'

She looked out at the rain, which had progressed from light drizzle to a regular downpour. Already the grass was soggy and puddles were starting to form on the metalled drive.

'Please. Instead of going to a pub we could talk at my house,' she suggested.

Connor moved broad shoulders. 'Wherever. Give me ten minutes,' he said, and went back amongst the remaining members of the crew to answer queries here, check that a task had been remembered there and generally cast an eagle eye over the clearing up.

Why had she issued her invitation? Jennet wondered as engines roared into life and trucks started to trundle past down the drive. Although she welcomed family and friends into her home, she was not in the habit of opening the door to single men. Let alone to a single man who had taken up such disturbing residence in her thoughts. But now the two of them were destined to be alone together. Again, she fretted. And? And nothing. All they were involved in was a business discussion.

Ten minutes later, the archway was empty and the last of the convoy of vehicles had disappeared, with the janitor bringing up the rear in a hiccuping yellow three-wheeler.

'I'm parked around the back,' Connor said, and frowned out at the rain. 'If you'd like to wait here—'

'It's OK, I'll come with you.' She held her folder up over her head. 'This'll protect me.'

He looked dubious. 'You're sure?'

'Positive.'

'We go that-a-way,' he said, jerking a thumb to the left along the front of the building. 'I suggest we run. Ready?'

She nodded and they sprinted out together. As the rain lashed at her face, Jennet screwed up her eyes. Standing in the dry, she had not properly realised how much heavier the downpour had become and the folder made a poor umbrella.

Side by side, they careered around the corner of the school and sped through the gardens. Rain speared down in relentless rods from the sky and bounced up from the ground like pellets. Reaching a maze of fabricated bungalows which bore door plaques declaring 'SCIENCE LABORATORY', 'ART ROOM', 'WOODWORK SHOP' and such, they cut between them.

She smeared a drip from her chin. 'How much further?' she panted.

'Just past the Cadet Training Corps hut.'

'Thank goodness, I'm— Yikes!'

She had been looking ahead, but a puddle the size of a miniature lake was immediately in front of her. Launching herself up into a valiant leap, she landed with two sneakered feet a few inches from the far edge. She landed flat-footed and at an angle, which meant that water shot out in a soaring upward plank. It shot out at Connor who was alongside her. A few drops spattered onto his sweatshirt before the plank of water crumpled and landed with a great splash.

''Struth!' he exclaimed.

Jennet looked out from beneath the folder to see that his jeans were dark-soaked and dripping. From mid-thigh down to the ankles, he was drenched. Laughter bubbled. For him to have been doused seemed like an apt punishment for shouting at her. It was divine—and comical—retribution.

'I'm sorry,' she said, smothering her laughter and being determinedly straight-faced. 'I never—'

'Leave it,' he rapped, and sped off, this time keeping noticeably ahead of her.

Reaching the car, he unlocked the passenger door and strode around to open his own. He was climbing into his seat, when she tumbled in beside him.

'What comes next?' he demanded, furiously swiping straggles of dark wet hair from his eyes.

'Excuse me?'

'First you mess up filming, then you subject me to your own personal Niagara. And it's not funny!'

'That all depends on where you're sitting,' Jennet replied, then became dutifully repentant. 'No, no, it's not.'

He glowered. 'These things come in threes, so it's two down and one to go,' he declared. 'What other trip-wire do you have lying in wait for me?'

'None. Splashing you was an accident—'

'Splashing? You damn near *drowned* me!'

'Like my walking into the line of the camera was an accident,' she persisted. 'And I'm sorry.'

'So it's just my bad luck that I'm doomed to spend the rest of the day wearing wet and soggy trousers?' he enquired, picking tetchily at the doused denim. 'It's my bad luck if I'm doomed to end up with the flu or arthritis or—'

'You're not doomed to anything,' she cut in. 'When we get to my house, which is no more than a ten-minute drive away, you can take off your jeans and—'

'Take them off?' he protested.

'Your sweatshirt too, if you wish, and I'll put them both into the tumble-drier.' She flashed a synthetic smile. 'Don't be scared; I shall keep a tight rein on my free-floating lust and I promise not to rape you.'

Connor slung her a dark look. 'That's a relief.' He switched on the ignition, boosted the heater and set the windscreen-wipers in motion. 'How do we get to your place?'

'For a start, when we go out of the school gates you turn left.'

As they drove down the drive, Jennet untied the sleeves of her sweater and pulled it free from her shoulders. His jeans might be saturated, but she was wet too. The front of her T-shirt was damp, there were dark splodges on her trousers, and diamond droplets sparkled amongst the cotton-knit.

'If you had stripped off your T-shirt we would've needed to show the episode after the nine o'clock watershed,' he remarked. 'And viewing figures wouldn't just have soared, they'd have sky-rocketed.'

'What do you mean?' she asked.

'I mean you're not wearing a bra.'

She glanced down. With the disappearance of the sun, the temperature had fallen. The car heater had yet to take effect, she was cold and her nipples had risen like two stiff thimbles, lifting the damp white cloth. She fought an urge to cross her arms over her chest. Admittedly it was difficult not to notice the flagrantly proud points and the shadow of wine-dark aureoles, but did he have to comment?

'Perhaps you've dispensed with all items of underwear?' Connor continued.

A minute or two ago he had been angry, but now his look had become amused and his tone was bantering. On balance, his anger seemed easier to handle, Jennet thought, but she would not fall to pieces.

'No, I'm wearing a pair of kanga briefs, high-cut and scanty,' she replied, with a cool she did not feel.

A grin tweaked the corners of his mouth. 'Thank you for sharing that with me. How about material and colour? A little more information would help for when I'm mentally undressing you.'

'You mentally undress me?' she enquired.

'In my idle moments, as I'm sure plenty of other guys do. Are the briefs made of black silk?' he continued. 'Or perhaps scarlet satin and trimmed with tassels?'

'They're georgette and in a leopardskin print,' she informed him, with studied nonchalance. 'We go left at the crossroads, then keep straight on across the valley and up the hill on the other side.'

'Thanks,' he replied and, to her relief, fell quiet.

Six weeks ago, Jennet had accused him of thinking she was prim and proper, Connor recalled as he drove along the high-hedged country road, and she had referred to it again today. She was mistaken. He didn't. No one prim and proper could write the kind of adventurous, cutting-edge dialogue which she wrote or create such quirky characters. Or wear leopard-printed briefs. Or kiss him the way she had, a sly inner voice added.

He frowned out through the windscreen. She had verve and a feisty spirit. It was rare that people battled against him the way she did and whilst her battling must create havoc with his blood-pressure levels he found it refreshing. And sexy. Contrarily, he got a kick out of their fights.

Yet Jennet was also...contained, he brooded. There was something tantalisingly elusive about her and he had a sense of a lot going on inside her which she preferred to keep to herself.

'What inspired you to write for television?' he asked, thinking how little he knew about her.

'I used to work in advertising as a copywriter. Seven or eight years ago the agency was commissioned to make a television commercial and—'

'For what?'

'Spaghetti hoops.'

'Not the one where the hoops sang and did a tap dance across the table while the father and the little boy watched on?' he said.

Jennet nodded. 'You remember it?'

'Yes, it's always stuck in my mind because at the time my—' He stopped short. 'I remember it.'

'I wrote the words for the song.'

' "If you want your taste buds to swoon, try a few of us on your spoon," ' Connor sang. He grinned at her. 'I didn't realise you were so multi-talented.'

'It's hardly Cole Porter,' she protested.

'More like Sondheim,' he said, and she laughed.

He had not noticed it before, but she had a very sexy laugh. It started off as a giggle, but changed somewhere between her throat and her mouth to emerge as a low chuckle. His eyes dipped to her breasts and the pert twin buttons of her nipples. She also had a honey of a figure. He shifted in his seat. It must be because he hadn't made love in a long time, but he could feel himself becoming aroused. Like some over-eager and callow youth, he thought impatiently.

'Anyhow, the glimpse into the world of television set me thinking,' Jennet continued. 'When I was a teenager I was forever tucked away in corners scribbling all kinds of stories, then in my twenties I switched to humorous articles—'

'Were any of them published?'

'Quite a few. And I decided to try and write a play for television. You go left at this T-junction. My first two efforts were rejected, but according to the script editor the third possessed potential. Mind you, it took her six months to write back and she required hefty changes, but by that time I was married so I never made them.'

'You stopped writing when you got married?' he said as he halted at the junction. 'Why?'

She straightened the sweater on her lap. 'There were other things to do. But I still had ideas and after Stuart was killed—'

'Your husband was killed?' Connor cut in, in surprise.

'In a road accident.'

'I'm sorry,' he said. He looked both ways along the quiet country lane before turning the corner. 'I didn't know.'

'It was...traumatic. Getting my life back on track took time, but when I did I started to write again. I wrote *Hutton's Spa* and the rest, as they say, is history.'

'You gave up working at the agency—when?'

'As soon as I received the first cheque from Ensign. Advertising had become samey and I was pleased to leave—even though writing for a living can be risky.'

'What made you decide to write about a health farm?' he asked.

Jennet grinned. 'My stepfather. Freddie isn't the son of an earl like Dinsdale, but he was once the part-owner of a health hydro and he used to tell me tales about it. About the staff and the clients.'

'Used to tell tales? Past tense?'

'Freddie and my mother were divorced—oh, around sixteen years ago. See the lane on the right beside the little church?' she said, gesturing ahead. 'I live directly opposite.'

The house was nineteenth century, built of red brick and faced with decorative panels of flint. Virginia creeper clambered up the walls, curled around the windows, waved hopeful strands towards the grey slated roof. The chimneys were tall and twisted. A well stood in the white-fenced front garden.

'A house with character,' Connor appraised, with a smile.

'It was originally the home of a blacksmith and the forge which stood beside it is now my garage,' Jennet told him. 'You can park outside the front gate.'

They climbed out into the rain and hurried up a stone-flagged path to the front door.

'Come in,' she said, leading the way through a tiny hall and into the living room.

With white walls, dark oak beams and an inglenook fireplace, the room was cosy. A patterned ruby carpet covered the floor and rich ruby curtains hung at the windows. Gleaming horse brasses were pinned to one of the beams, while a row of bright pottery fishes decorated another. Her lead-crystal beaver had pride of place on a corner shelf.

Taking a box of matches from a bureau, Jennet struck one and put it to the logs which sat in an iron basket. The match caught the tinder and orange flames licked up.

'The room'll soon be warm. If you come upstairs, I'll find you a dressing gown and you can take off your wet clothes,' she said.

Connor arched a brow. 'You don't want me sitting around in my underwear so that you can ogle?'

'Thanks, but I'll pass,' she said quickly.

'Your choice,' he replied, and followed her back into the hall and up the narrow staircase.

On the landing, she stopped. 'I'll get the dressing gown and—' she indicated a door on the right '—you can change in the spare room. I won't be a moment.'

Going into her room, Jennet sped across to the wardrobe and began to riffle through. Maybe it was because she was out of practice with male/female repartee, but his talk of sitting in his underwear had sent her imagination into overdrive again. She took a deep breath. Grow up, she told herself. Behave.

'Here you are,' she said, returning to the landing to hand him a navy towelling robe.

Connor held it up. 'This belonged to your husband?' he asked.

'No, it's mine.'

'But it's a man's size.'

'Freddie bought it for me last Christmas and whenever he buys clothes they're always either much too small or far too big.'

'He still gives you presents?'

She nodded. 'We don't meet so often now because he lives in Canada, but we're still fond of each other and always will be.' She turned towards her room. 'I'll see you downstairs.'

Stripping off her damp clothes, Jennet drew on a bra, a long, loose cream woollen sweater and dark brown leggings. Brown soft leather flatties replaced her sodden

sneakers. She combed her hair, made a face at herself
in the mirror and went down to the living room.

She was poking at the blazing logs when Connor came
in, his wet jeans and sweatshirt draped over one arm.
As she glanced back at him, the breath snagged in her
throat. In the towelling robe and barefoot, he looked
casual, at home and alarmingly virile. The robe might
be man size, yet it was a couple of sizes too small for
him, which meant that it revealed more than was intended. A sexy excess. The wrists which protruded from
the too short sleeves were broad. The legs which could
be seen from just above the knee down were strong and
well muscled. In the deep V, his chest was bare and
sprinkled with whorls of coarse dark hair.

'I'll put your things in the drier,' she yammered, suddenly aware that she *was* ogling. She took the clothes
from him. 'They shouldn't take many minutes. Would
you like a drink?' she called as she went out through the
hall and into the kitchen. 'Coffee, tea, or something
alcoholic?'

Connor followed her, to stand in the doorway with a
shoulder resting against the jamb. 'It's been a long day
and I could murder a gin and tonic.'

'I'll have one too.' She inserted the clothes and acti-
vated the machine. 'With ice and lemon?'

'Please. I want to apologise for shouting at you for
getting in the camera line,' he said as she took crystal
tumblers from a cupboard and started to prepare their
drinks. 'I went a little bit over the top.'

'You went loads over, with bells ringing and claxons
blaring!' Jennet protested.

'OK, but after lousing up half a dozen times Henry
had finally got it right and then—'

'I appeared.'

He gave a lopsided smile. 'And I went berserk. I'm not too good at humility, but—'

'Your apology is accepted,' she said, and handed him his glass.

'Thanks. I like your home,' Connor said, his gaze travelling around the small kitchen with its scrubbed pine units, the dried flowers which she had pinned to a beam, the cow-faced clock. He went across to look out of the window at a patio where rain fell on tubs planted with daffodils and tulips, and the green lawn beyond. 'Living in an apartment you get to hanker after a garden and a garage.'

She tipped a bag of dry-roasted peanuts into a wooden bowl. 'Where is your apartment?'

'Hammersmith. It's on the third floor and overlooks the river, so I have great views. But there's nowhere private where I can sit outdoors if it's sunny and sometimes it's impossible to find a parking space and I have to leave my car streets away. How long have you been here?' he asked, going with her back into the living room.

'Two years,' she said as they sat down in ruby and green velvet armchairs in front of the fire. 'Peanuts?'

'Please.' He helped himself to a handful and chewed for a moment or two. 'So you didn't live here with your husband?'

Jennet looked at the fire. Flames danced, the logs glowed red and heat was spreading.

'No. At first we rented a house, then we bought a new one in a village a few miles away. It was spacious, with all the luxury extras, but—'

'It had too many memories?' Connor suggested, when she broke off to frown.

'Yes.'

'It can be difficult to throw off memories,' he said, as though he had suffered similar difficulties himself.

She nodded and took a quick sip from her glass. 'I finished this episode today,' she said, opening the damp-edged folder and passing him a sheaf of papers clipped together. A smile curved her lips. 'It's poignant and moving, but it has a comic element.'

'You decided my idea wasn't so "icky" after all?' he enquired.

'Sorry?'

'Beth and Craig.'

She stared. 'I haven't written about them. I've written about a woman who comes to the health farm to lose weight and goes into labour. Much to her surprise and everyone else's. I gave you the outline in February.'

'Beth and Craig get heavy in the next episode?' Connor demanded.

'They don't get heavy at all.'

His eyes took on a metallic glint. 'But I assumed that because you'd quit arguing you'd seen reason.'

'Ditto,' Jennet said. He swore loud and long, but she steadily held his gaze. 'There appears to have been a breakdown in communication.'

'You appear to have laid down a third trip-wire!' he retorted, waving the script around.

'It isn't a trip-wire. It's a killer of an episode, so there's no need to start bouncing off the walls,' she protested. 'Connor, I've made all the decisions about plots since the series began and—'

'You reckon you're infallible?'

'No, but the series is attracting excellent audiences.'

'You said you had deep respect for my creative judgement,' he reminded her brusquely.

'I do, but I also said a toyboy affair was no go and—well, I am doing something right.'

'You can do something even better,' he grated. 'Hell, all I'm asking for is a romance, not an episode set in a third-degree burns unit or featuring mutant killer slugs.'

'Even so—'

'Check out any successful television series and you'll find that, sooner or later, there is always love interest. Always,' he pronounced, slapping his hand down flat like a blade on the arm of his chair and making her jump. 'People like it, so buy into it.'

'I don't want to and I see no need to,' she declared, and rose from her chair. 'Your clothes should be ready by now.'

In the kitchen, Jennet stopped the tumble-drier and pulled out his jeans. Her assumption that his silence meant his assent had been naïve, she thought as she shook them out. She should have guessed he would still wish to impose his will. But she would resist. A shiver zigzagged through her. She must.

'Your jeans are dry,' she said as Connor appeared. She inspected his sweatshirt. 'And so is this.'

He took the clothes from her and placed them on the table. 'Why are you being so bloody-minded?' he demanded. Stepping forward, he clasped two long-fingered hands around her waist and yanked her towards him. 'Is this some kind of power play?'

Jennet swallowed. To be so close to a man, a virile, sexy man who, beneath his robe, was almost naked, disturbed her. A feeling of imminent excitement clogged the breath in her throat. She felt a tingle of need—a need to touch his chest and move her fingers across the coarse dark hair.

'Power play?' she asked, and heard her voice sound reedy and strained.

'Are you getting too big for your bootees and getting an attitude? Have you decided that because you've been successful it's time *you* called the shots? All of them?'

'You think I'm that kind of person?' she said indignantly.

He frowned. 'No, as a matter of fact I don't, but—'

'And I'm not.'

'Then how about being a tub-thumping feminist who needs to demonstrate her superiority to a mere male?' he enquired.

Jennet gave a tight smile. ' "Mere male" is not the way I'd describe you, but—'

'How would you describe me?' he cut in.

'Words like big and bolshie and overbearing spring to mind.'

'How about right?'

'No! But I'm not a feminist.'

'So we're back to sheer bloody-mindedness.' He cast her an impatient look. 'What do I have to do to get you to agree to include an affair between Beth and Craig?' he demanded.

'There's nothing you can do,' she replied.

She made to step back, but his hands tightened and he drew her closer.

'And you'd like me to drop the subject?'

'Please.' Foolish things were happening in the pit of her stomach and she would also have liked him to release *her*.

'Just please?' Connor said. 'You don't intend to use your womanly wiles to persuade me to see things your way? You're not going to pucker up your lips and kiss me again?'

Jennet swallowed. She could feel the heat from his body, feel his fingers hard at her waist, feel a *throb* in the air. She had always considered him to be relaxed, but despite his teasing tone he did not seem so relaxed now. Indeed, the slumberous darkening of his grey eyes indicated that he was as affected by her proximity as she was by his.

'*I* didn't kiss *you* before,' she protested.

'You damn well did.'

'No, it was mutual.'

'Look, sweetheart, you invited me to—'

'Telephone,' she announced brightly, and oh, so thankfully, as the phone rang in the living room.

Connor stepped back. 'I'll go and change,' he said, as if the interruption had come as something of a relief for him, too, and he picked up his clothes and strode swiftly off upstairs.

'How's my hotshot daughter?' a smoky voice asked, when she answered.

'Fit and well,' she replied. 'And you?'

'Hunky-dory. You sound sort of... breathless.'

'With rushing to the phone,' she claimed.

'A reporter's rung me from *The Comet*,' her mother continued, her words crackling down the international telephone wire.

'Asking about me?'

'Yes, but I was the soul of discretion. Whatever he said, my reply was "No comment." No comment when he asked which line of work were you in. No comment when—'

Tina was cheerily detailing her repeated replies when footsteps sounded on the stairs and Connor appeared in the doorway. He was fully dressed.

She put her hand over the mouthpiece. 'I'll be with you in a minute.'

'Don't bother. I must go,' he said, baring a wrist to check the time and frowning.

'OK.' Jennet reached for the script which he had discarded and thrust it at him. 'But read this. Read it!' she insisted, when he seemed reluctant.

'So you've no need to worry,' her mother said, into her ear.

'Sorry?'

'About *The Comet* learning anything from me.'

'Oh, right.'

'Thanks for the drink. I'll let myself out,' Connor said, and disappeared. A moment later, the front door banged shut behind him.

'You had a visitor?' Tina enquired.

'Connor Malone. He's the director of *Hutton's Spa*.'

'You've been . . . entertaining him?' There was a trill of laughter. 'So that's why you were breathless.'

'There was no entertaining,' she declared, fully aware of what the word meant in her mother's dictionary. 'We were discussing my scripts, that's all.'

'What's this Connor Malone like?'

Jennet gave an impatient sigh. 'Tall, dark and handsome.'

'Married?'

'No.'

'Gay?'

'Definitely not. How's Mitch?'

Now it was her mother who sighed impatiently. 'We're going through a rocky patch, though—' she chuckled '—the making up is always fun. You need a man about the house,' she continued, 'and tall, dark and handsome sounds ideal.'

'Not to me,' Jennet responded, and moved the conversation on to more general, less alarming subjects.

When she put down the telephone, she walked across to the window. She stared bleakly out at the rain. Connor had once asked if she had a special reason for being so hostile towards the idea of a Beth-with-Craig fling. She did. Writing about a fictional older woman/younger man affair would come too close to real life.

It would resurrect fears which had once slashed like a knife into her heart and ripped through her soul. Fears which had made her *bleed*. Collecting up the glasses, Jennet took them through to the kitchen. Her wounds had healed and she refused to open them up again.

CHAPTER FOUR

'JENNET hasn't changed her mind about Beth and Craig making whoopee?' Lester enquired.

'Not yet,' Connor replied curtly.

Resting his elbows on the desk, he placed his hands together and steepled his fingers. He frowned. Ever since he had exited from her house a fortnight ago, he had been waiting for her to ring and say, guess what? She had had second thoughts, seen sense and was busily embroiled in the desired script. He had waited in vain. And the longer he had waited, the more determined he had become to enforce his request.

'It isn't as though you're asking for anything unreasonable,' his companion said, echoing his thoughts.

'On the contrary. Now that the characters have been established, we need something meatier, something which'll add strength to the programme and provide continuity. We need a romance—dammit!—but she's not having any. So far.'

'You'll have to call her in and read the riot act. Smartish. Lay it on the line that we've had enough of this pussyfooting around and tell her it's time for her to do the business.'

Leaning back in his swivel chair, Connor swung slowly from side to side. 'I guess,' he agreed.

The chairman smiled. His executive producer might be frowning, but he had seen how when he acted tough people always obeyed, which meant the crisis was as good as over.

'You're happy to leave the next shoot at Hammingden School until the summer holidays?' Lester said, dismissing the problem from his mind and moving on.

'I am.'

'I had my headmaster pal, Bill, on the phone earlier this afternoon and that's what I told him. He was wondering if you wanted to spend a day or two there at half-term.'

'No need. Filming for *Hutton's Spa* is ahead of schedule.'

'Which gives you the opportunity to take a break. Make it soon. You haven't had any time off since heaven knows when and—' Lester peered across the desk '—you look kind of stressed.'

'I'll think about it,' he said.

'Bill was telling me that I'd once met Stuart Galbraith, Jennet's husband,' the older man continued conversationally. 'I'd forgotten because at the time there was no link to be made and no reason to remember, but a few years ago the guy made up a golf foursome when I was partnering Bill in Sussex.'

Lester liked to come down to Connor's first-floor office and chat. As splendid as his own abode was, and as much as he enjoyed surfing the channels on his bank of televisions and zapping into everything available, it did tend to be a touch quiet, a touch remote. But down here in the comfortably untidy room, with its crammed bookshelves and paper-piled desk, something was always happening. People popped in to consult the executive producer on one point or other, poked their heads around the door to impart snippets of information, came and went along the corridor. Here there was a vibrancy.

Connor stopped his swinging. 'What was he like?' he enquired.

'Blond and clean-cut. Personable young bloke, but—' Lester snapped the scarlet leather-braided braces which held his trousers aloft over his rotund paunch '—a stickler for marking down the number of shots we took on our golf cards and playing to the rules.'

'You mean he wouldn't let you cheat?' came the dry suggestion.

The chairman guffawed. 'I mean he was too particular. I know I only met him the once and didn't take much notice, but I'm surprised he appealed to Jennet,' he continued. 'She's a live wire, whereas he came over as... a bit stuffy.'

'Stuffy to a way-out individual like yourself maybe, but entirely sensible to the rest of us.'

He guffawed again. 'Could be.'

'And Jennet doesn't appear to have bothered with anyone else since he died,' Connor remarked, 'so the guy must've had something.'

A knock sounded on the door and his middle-aged secretary came into the room. 'Your letters to be signed,' she told him, placing a file on his desk.

As the woman disappeared, Lester rose to his feet. 'I suppose I'd better go and deal with my correspondence too,' he said reluctantly.

His statement about Jennet not bothering with any other man had been incorrect, Connor thought cryptically as he started to scrawl his name in a bold black signature. The sparks which now seemed to fly whenever they were alone together indicated that her sexual drive was in good working order—even if she would have preferred it otherwise. Even if she had no desire for a love affair.

To be widowed so young and so tragically must have been harrowing, he mused, yet she had recovered. Her recovery would have been helped by the fact that she seemed so secure in herself as a person, so well adjusted. He scowled. She might be well adjusted, but she was also exasperatingly stubborn. Lester seemed to believe he could wave a magic wand and she would meekly comply with his demands. As if.

After signing the final letter, he screwed the top back onto his fountain-pen. He was becoming obsessed with her refusal to produce the required script—which was why, as well as apparently looking stressed, he felt stressed. And ready to commit murder. Or hari-kari.

Connor closed the folder. He was also becoming obsessed with the woman herself. Jennet seemed to be forever in his mind, especially at night: her gurgling laugh, her tempting figure with those erect nipples...and that kiss. It annoyed the hell out of him.

Jennet gazed up at the traffic lights. 'Change,' she implored, but they shone a steady, unblinking red.

She had come into Central London to buy air tickets and traveller's cheques, been struck by a brainwave of an idea and, on impulse, had decided to drive out to the television centre and announce her idea to Connor. But rush-hour traffic had begun to gather and progress was slow. She thumped a fist on the steering wheel. Frustratingly slow. If she did not get there within the next twenty minutes, chances were he would have left and her journey would be wasted.

As she waited at the junction, her gaze swung to a newsagent's shop where 'puller' posters for morning and evening papers were displayed outside. FAMOUS TENNIS STAR IN DRUG-POPPING SCANDAL! screamed *The Comet's* board. 'Come *on*,' she muttered. Today, like every day for the past fortnight, she had bought a copy of *The Comet* and the hysterically reported scandal was an unproved rumour of one-off years-ago pill-taking and a fuss about nothing.

The campaign to identify her had been a fuss about nothing, too. Whilst regular bids for information had been made throughout the first week, come the second the subject had been ignored. It seemed that no one had contacted the journalist and no friends or acquaintances had contacted her, either, to say they had read of his quest. Jennet grinned. The campaign had fallen flat. The danger had gone.

'Thank you, thank you,' she burbled as the lights flashed green, and pressed her foot down hard on the accelerator.

A quarter of an hour later, she swung onto the vast forecourt of the Ensign television complex, swiftly parked and sped towards the entrance. Pushing around revolving doors, she burst into the marble-floored foyer.

'Do you know whether Mr Malone is still here?' she asked the smart young blonde who was sitting behind the reception desk.

'Think so. Would you like me to ring and—?'

'Don't bother, thanks. I'll go straight up,' she said, and, bypassing the lift as too time-consuming, she headed for the stairs.

Reaching the wide, first-floor corridor, she jogged along past a series of polished walnut doors until she came to one emblazoned with a brass panel bearing the words 'EXECUTIVE PRODUCER'. She brushed stray tendrils of hair from her brow and straightened her shoulders. Now that she had arrived, the prospect of seeing Connor again was making the nerves jump beneath her skin. 'Pathetic!' she muttered, chastising herself, and gulped in a breath and knocked.

'Come in,' a familiarly deep voice called.

'Sorry to be at the last—last minute, but I—I need to talk to you,' Jennet panted as she entered.

Connor frowned. He had been thinking about her and for her suddenly to materialise in the flesh was disconcerting. She looked good in the flesh. Very good. She was wearing a cream silk shirt with a caramel-coloured suede waistcoat and matching soft suede trousers. Her face was flushed and her high breasts impetuously rose and fell. She had been hurrying.

'Likewise,' he said curtly. 'But you go first.'

Now seemed as good a time as any to tell her she must stop being a complete pain in the butt and do as he asked, yet he was wary of the inevitable collision.

'There are two things,' she said, and needed to gulp in another breath. He had leant back in his chair, his legs splayed and with every taut inch reeking of testosterone. 'One, I'm willing to have an affair.'

'You are?'

Jennet nodded energetically. 'I don't want to cause any trouble or miss out on possibilities and I know how keen you are, so I'm happy to go ahead. OK?'

'Sounds like an offer I can't refuse,' Connor replied.

She heard the underlying note of humour, saw his slow grin, the gleam in his eyes, and became aware of how her words had emerged. A traitorous excitement speared through her. The idea of having an affair with him did have its attractions. Potent attractions. But there was also a downside.

'I think I'd better rephrase that,' she said.

His smile deepened the indentations in his cheeks. 'I think you had.'

'I'm willing to put a love affair into *Hutton's Spa*.'

He laughed and rose to his feet. He had been certain they were heading for a fall-out, but he had been wrong. The stalemate had been resolved. Now the series could reach its full potential. And now he did not have to tell her the action which he had decided he must take—would have been *forced* to take if she had refused to co-operate—and face the possible consequences.

'Great!' he declared, and, walking out from behind his desk, he wrapped his arms around her and kissed her.

Caught up in his delight, Jennet kissed him back—spontaneously and wholeheartedly. Her lips parted on his and she felt the graze of his tongue, his teeth, the silken confines of his mouth. Her head started to spin. This was what she had fantasised about in those reckless, foolish moments, she realised dimly. Connor kissing her, his mouth eager and searching, the feel of his body against hers.

When the kiss broke and moved into another, there was a subtle change of mood. Delight deepened into desire. Into need. His hand trailed gently along the column of her throat and down, sliding over the swell of her breast and inside her waistcoat to close over the firm curve. At the circling of his fingers on her burgeoning nipple, she stirred restlessly. If only she were not wearing a shirt and a bra. If only she could feel his touch on her naked breasts.

She had one hand at his waist and, as he had moved, the navy sweatshirt he wore had ridden up and her fingers were touching bare hidden flesh. Flesh which was smooth and warm and seductive. Her fingertips prickled. She longed to slide her hand beneath the heavy navy cotton and up over the flatness of his stomach to his chest. She longed to feel the wiry hair and explore the flat discs of his nipples.

Murmuring something incoherent against her mouth, Connor shifted, his hands travelling down her back to cup the roundness of her buttocks in the soft suede trousers and pull her into him.

As she felt the thrust of his manhood against her thighs, her senses reeled. The tips of her breasts tightened in a pleasure-pain and an ache throbbed in her groin. She had slept alone for so long. Too long.

You want me, Jennet thought, and I want you. I want you to make love to me. So very much. Now.

Abruptly wrenching his mouth from hers, Connor placed his hands on her waist and steered her away. He stepped back, breaking contact.

'Not the place,' he said, breathing heavily. 'Not the time.'

She stared. For one confused, horror-stricken moment she thought she must have spoken out loud—even *begged* him to make love to her—then she, too, became aware of the footsteps which sounded outside in the corridor and were coming closer.

'Just popped in to say I'm leaving,' Lester announced, his head appearing around the door a moment later. When he saw her, he smiled. 'What a nice surprise. Have you and Connor got it together?'

Jennet looked at him with dazed green eyes. 'Got it together?' she echoed.

What did he mean? she wondered. The chairman had not seen them locked in each other's arms, but could he have guessed? She raised her fingers to lips which felt softly bruised and thoroughly kissed. The evidence was there.

'Everything's agreed,' Connor said. 'Jennet will be writing in a romance.' He grinned at her. 'Yes?'

'Erm—' She cleared her throat. 'Yes.'

She might be knocked askew and out of sync, but he had spoken easily. He had recovered his composure in what seemed like two seconds flat. She cast him a veiled look. Even though he had reneged on his intention to keep her at arm's length, the fast cooling of his emotions suggested that he did not rate their embrace as too much of an event. Which, she thought stingingly, was only to be expected from a man with his romantic track record.

'Excellent,' Lester declared, coming into the room. 'The romance'll feature in the next episode which you write?'

She hesitated. The conversation was moving on too quickly and there was something which she needed to explain.

'You'll start work on it straight away?' the chairman demanded.

Feeling pressurised, she nodded. 'I will, and that brings me to the second thing which I have to tell you,' she said, speaking to Connor. 'At the weekend I'm flying out to Capri and expect to be away for two or three weeks. However, I shall be working every day—'

'Magical island, Capri,' Lester cut in. 'My wife and I have visited a couple of times. Which hotel will you be staying at?'

'I'm not staying in a hotel. I own a small villa there,' she explained.

'Lucky girl. You go often?'

'Usually for the month of June and again in October, and I rent the house out to holidaymakers, as and when, for the rest of the year. But this morning the management company which looks after the property rang to say there'd been a heavy storm which'd caused some damage.'

'Shame,' he said, clicking his tongue in sympathy.

'They asked if I could fly out to see what repairs I felt were necessary, agree prices and be present when the workmen are around. There're some holiday bookings arranged for the summer, so things have to be fixed. I shall continue to write,' she said, turning to Connor again, 'and I'm at the end of the telephone. There isn't a fax, but—'

'How many bedrooms do you have?' the chairman interrupted.

'Three. Two upstairs and one down. Why?' she asked. 'Are you interested in renting the villa?'

'No thanks, my wife and I prefer the luxury of hotels. But I was thinking that you could take Connor with you.'

'Connor?' she protested.

She shot him a look and saw that he was as startled— and as appalled—by the suggestion as she.

Lester nodded. 'It'd make working together so much simpler and the poor guy needs a holiday.'

'I don't think he'd like a holiday in Capri,' Jennet said hastily. 'The villa is away from the town and very quiet.'

'And I have too much happening here to take time off right now,' Connor declared.

'You always have too much happening,' the older man complained, half-jokily, and walked to the door. 'Time I departed.'

As he left, Connor strode back around his desk to gather up papers and place them in a red wire basket.

'I'm off home too,' he said, and grinned. 'Thanks for agreeing to Beth and Craig combining. You made the right decision. It'll be—'

'The romance isn't between Beth and Craig,' Jennet cut in. 'You didn't give me the chance to say, but it's between Beth and Dinsdale.'

He had crossed to close a drawer in a filing cabinet and now he slammed it shut. 'You are the most singularly perverse woman I have ever met,' he declared.

'And it's a love affair which doesn't actually happen.'

He looked at her. 'Wowee,' he drawled.

Her temper flared. 'You know,' she said, 'sometimes I really hate you.'

'Only sometimes? I am honoured.'

'The realisation that they love each other sneaks up and takes them both unawares,' she persevered as Connor opened the office door and they went out into the corridor.

'I'm supposed to be filled with wonder?'

'You're supposed to listen and then let the idea marinate for five minutes,' she shot back.

He lifted a brow. '*Touché*. Please explain.'

'The emotion is strong and true, but they fight it because Dinsdale is married. All right, his relationship with his wife is of the jog-along type and could be ended, but he discovers feelings of integrity.'

'Dinsdale does?' he protested. 'Dinsdale the cad?'

'Yes. He realises that his marriage matters to him and after much agonising—which can become a "will they, won't they?" struggle and maintained over several episodes—he decides he must remain faithful. It'll have far more angst than an affair between Beth and Craig. Far more poignant yearning of forbidden love. What do you think?'

They had reached the stairs and Connor set off down them. He rarely used the lift. Walking whenever he could, plus swimming regularly and working out in a gym, meant he kept in trim.

'I don't know,' he said, frowning.

'The idea came to me this afternoon out of the blue, but it's a good one,' she insisted, needing to hurry to keep pace with him. 'Caring and sharing are the "in" themes of today. We may be approaching the end of the decade, but you must wake up and "smell the nineties," as someone once said.'

'Who?'

Jennet scrunched up her brow. 'I think it was some guy in a *Die Hard* movie.'

'The one who kills three hundred people in ten minutes without breaking into a sweat?' He gave her a dry look. 'Well, in that case...'

'Putting Beth and Dinsdale through the wringer of love is perfection. It *is*,' she declared as they walked across the lobby. 'Connor, I'm offering you the love interest which'll keep the viewers gripped.'

He pursed his lips. 'Maybe.'

'For definite!'

He stood aside to allow her to go ahead of him out through the revolving doors. 'Tell you what,' he said as they emerged into the open air, 'write a first draft of an episode and I'll see what I think.'

Jennet gave him an impatient look, then nodded. His response was a long way from the enthusiasm which she had hoped for, but at least he had not issued a straight-out veto.

'I'll put the script which I've started to one side,' she told him, 'and as soon as I'm installed on Capri I'll get busy with Beth and Dinsdale.'

'You'll keep me informed on progress?'

'Every few days and I'll send you the draft as soon as possible.' She noticed a small gang of pressmen gathered beside the entrance on the far right-hand side of the car park. 'Are they waiting for someone special?' she asked.

'I believe that an American politician who's rumoured to be a hot tip for next President is coming to be interviewed for a current affairs programme,' he replied. 'Where are you parked?'

'Over beside the wall,' she said, pointing to the left.

'And me.'

As they set off along gap-toothed rows of stationary vehicles, there was a sudden shout from amidst the group at the distant entrance. Jennet looked back. A chubby young man with cropped gingery hair, wearing a black leather jacket and with a camera slung around his neck, was standing on tiptoe and waving. Waving in their direction.

'Jennet—Jennet Galbraith. Hi there,' he called, looking bright-eyed and eager.

'Fame at last,' Connor said wryly, beside her.

She stopped and frowned. 'Yes, but why?'

'I'm from *The Comet*,' the young man carolled.

Her blood ran cold. Ice-cold. 'And I thought I was safe,' she muttered.

'Just like a picture and a few words,' the young man yelled.

As he peeled away from the group and started off through the parked cars towards her, her stomach pitched and tossed. She felt ill.

'I don't want my photograph taken and I don't want to talk to him,' she told Connor, in a gabble. Flinging open her shoulder bag, she rooted feverishly for her car keys. 'I'm going.'

'OK, but wouldn't it make more sense to stay and—?'

'No!' she yelped.

'There's no reason to panic,' he started to protest, but she was already sprinting away.

She was much closer to her car than the photographer, Jennet thought thankfully as she ran, threading through parked vehicles, so she should be able to reach it, get in and drive out of the nearby exit before he had a chance to focus his camera.

'Jennet! Hey, Jennet, stop!' her pursuer called.

She shot a look back over her shoulder. The shout had sounded surprisingly close and, to her dismay, she saw that he was gaining on her. He might be carrying a good thirty pounds of excess weight, yet his membership of the paparazzi meant he had learned to move at speed.

'Keep going,' Connor instructed, coming up from behind to take hold of her arm and propel her along. 'Which is your car?'

'The silver-grey Fiesta,' she gasped.

'Just a picture for *The Comet*,' the photographer appealed.

She glanced back at him again. He was grinning and seemed to regard the chase as a game. Some game, she thought despairingly. If only he knew what was at stake.

'Leave me alone,' she implored, throwing the words over her shoulder as she ran. 'Please.'

'When ... I have ... one shot. Just one,' he panted.

'Can't you see that she doesn't want to be photographed?' Connor demanded.

'But ... she's a ... beaut. The readers'll ... love her.'

'Damn your readers, this is press harassment,' he shouted back, but the young man only chuckled.

As they reached her car, Jennet thrust the key into the lock and snatched open the door. She had scrambled inside and was switching on the engine when her pursuer suddenly leapt up like a jack-in-the-box at the front of the bonnet. He raised his camera.

'No!' she squawked, covering her face with both hands.

Connor slammed shut her door and strode forward. 'You're going to have to forget about a photograph,' he rasped.

As he advanced on him, the young man darted around the car and lifted his camera again. 'Who says?'

'I do,' he replied, walking around.

'You'll have to catch me first,' the photographer recited, sounding like a cheeky schoolboy, and cantered off to the far side.

'For heaven's sake,' Connor said impatiently, but he followed.

A circling began. Lowering her fingers, Jennet saw that Connor was steadily getting closer to her pursuer. She was wondering what he might do when he caught him and hoping it would not be anything too severe, when he suddenly stumbled, started to fall headlong, but recovered at the last moment.

'Dear God!' he said, standing upright and standing still. The colour had drained from his face and he was wincing.

The young man abandoned his canter. 'Are you all right?' he asked.

'What's the matter?' she enquired, climbing worriedly out of the car.

'I've hurt my leg.' Connor bent to spread his hand on his calf. 'It felt as if someone had taken a stick and whacked me as hard as they could. I didn't see stars, but it was close.' He tenderly felt the muscle. 'It's bloody painful.'

'You'll have ruptured your Achilles tendon,' the photographer proclaimed knowledgeably. 'Happened to me once. Agony, it was. You need to go to a hospital.'

'I'll take you,' Jennet said.

He shook his head. 'You have a long drive home—'

'You were hurt because you were helping me, so now I want to help you,' she told him, her voice firm. Going round to the passenger door, she opened it. 'Please, get in.'

Connor looked at her for a moment, then he sighed. 'Thanks.'

Holding onto the Fiesta and putting his weight onto his right leg, his good leg, he hobbled forward. Flinching, he manoeuvred himself awkwardly inside.

'Sorry to catch you on a bad-hair day,' the photographer said as Jennet made to return to the driver's side, 'though it looks fine to me.'

'I beg your pardon?' she said warily. He might no longer be wielding his camera, but it continued to hang around his neck.

'The reason you don't want to be photographed. Sorry if I upset you; didn't mean to. But congrats on the award.'

She frowned. 'I don't know what you're talking about.'

'The Best Writer gong which you've won.'

Her green eyes opened wide. 'I have?'

'For *Hutton's Spa*. Smashing series.'

'Thanks. And that's why you're here?'

'Nah, I've come to snap an American geezer—' he jerked back his head '—like the rest of the guys, but my office got premature wind of the award. I'm friendly with the receptionist here and when I quizzed her about you she told me you were around. She also said you were a looker and our readers are partial to a looker, so I thought—' He broke off. In the distance a limousine had arrived and the pressmen were surging around it. 'Must go. All the best with the leg, mate,' he said to Connor, and hurried off.

'Where's the nearest hospital?' Jennet asked as she drove towards the exit.

'If you turn left and go over the bridge, I'll direct you. You can drop me off at the emergency department,' Connor said, 'and I'll get a taxi to run me home.'

She shook her head. 'I shall take you.'

'But—'

'Don't argue.'

He gave a wan smile. 'No, ma'am.'

Jennet looked across at where Connor lay face down on an examination couch. They were in a side room off the consultant's office and his injury was being assessed.

'Jeans off,' a sergeant major of a nurse had matter-of-factly commanded, and he had stripped down to a pair of Mr Blobby—*Mr Blobby?*—boxer shorts.

Her eyes travelled along the length of his bare legs. They were firm-muscled and covered in a sprinkling of dark hair. He had a neat backside.

'Relax,' the white-coated consultant said as he kneaded probing fingers into the damaged lower limb.

'I am relaxed,' Connor protested, and grimaced. 'That hurts!'

'It will, because you've torn your calf muscle,' his tormentor declared. 'Your leg'll have to be put in plaster from just below the knee to the toes and set in the ballerina position.'

'Ballerina?' Jennet enquired.

The doctor smiled. 'The toes pointing down to enable the muscle to knit, Mrs Malone,' he explained. 'So your husband won't be able to put any weight on the leg.'

'Mrs Malone'? 'Your husband'? She shot Connor a look, expecting him to spout a denial and pungently set the man straight. But he said nothing. She glanced down at her left hand. She still wore her wedding ring, so the mistake was understandable.

'Rest your leg and keep it elevated. Keep moving your toes to maintain the circulation. Don't get the cast wet,' the consultant told him, and swung her another smile. 'Your husband's going to become frustrated by his lack of mobility, so expect a few tantrums.'

She shone a sweet smile at Connor. 'Will do.'

Why hadn't he corrected the doctor? she wondered. Did the idea of being regarded as married hold some appeal—though not married to her, just married in general? She recalled his remark about how difficult it was to throw off memories. Could that mean he continued to think about his marriage and his wife of long ago? Might he hanker after her? A hankering would explain why he had never replaced her.

'How long will I be in plaster?' Connor asked, pushing himself up on the couch and twisting round.

'At a guess, six weeks minimum.'

He muttered an oath.

'I'd like to see you in three weeks' time when we'll remove the cast to check on the healing process and give you another at an easier angle. Unfortunately we're running short of wheelchairs today,' the doctor continued, 'but I'm sure your wife will help you along to the plaster room. It's just down the corridor,' he explained, and smiled again at Jennet.

As the man returned to his office to attend to the next casualty, Connor struggled back into his jeans, socks and one shoe. Holding the spare, he slung an arm around her shoulders.

'Let's go,' he said, and with her supporting him around the waist he limped outside.

As they made their way slowly along the corridor, the ribbed waistband of his sweatshirt rode up again and Jennet found herself touching bare skin. She swallowed. To be in such close bodily contact might be necessary and public and mundane, yet it caused a basic jolt of reaction. An undeniable frisson. She could not help but be aware that, injured or not, Connor was still a powerful male animal.

'Why were you so desperate that the guy shouldn't take your picture?' he asked as they sat outside the plaster room with other patients, waiting for him to be called.

She hesitated, wondering if she should plead a bad-hair day, but decided that, given her frantic response and that her hair was freshly shampooed and shiny, it would not sound adequate.

'I'm not keen on being photographed by the Press so when I saw I was being chased and by someone from *The Comet*—' she made a face '—I just ran. Not the wisest course of action maybe,' she said lightly, 'but automatic.'

'Did he say why he wanted to photograph you?'

'It was because I've won the Best Writer Award.'

'Fantastic!' he exclaimed, smiling at her. 'Congratulations.'

'Thanks, and perhaps you'll be voted Best Director.'

'Who knows? You realise you'll be photographed by the Press at the awards ceremony?' Connor continued. 'In plenty.'

Jennet frowned. 'When is the ceremony?'

'It'll be in about six weeks' time. It's a grand dinner-jacket affair usually held at one of London's finest hotels. You may've seen it on television in the past.'

'The ceremony is televised?' she said, in alarm.

'Always. I don't much like being on the small screen, either,' he said, 'but—' He broke off as the door of the plaster room opened.

'Mr Malone?' said a technician.

'That's me,' he replied, and limped inside.

Jennet curled her fingers tight around the strap of her bag. She could not attend the awards ceremony. She dared not risk appearing on national television and being seen by the jogger who had been present when Stuart had been killed.

If the man saw her receiving the award and talked about how he'd witnessed an accident in which she was involved, perhaps word would eventually reach the media. People passed on any snippet of information in the hope of earning an easy shilling. Perhaps the media would interview the jogger, make further enquiries and, sooner or later, link her to her mother. Perhaps the man would then make sense of the quarrel which he had overheard. She drew in a shaky breath. The media—and in particular tabloids like *The Comet*—would have a field day.

Jennet frowned. 'Perhaps' featured strongly in her vision of catastrophe, so was she running too scared? Could this worst-case scenario be the product of an overly fertile imagination? Wouldn't she be wiser to resolutely push the whole thing from her mind?

She was telling herself to be positive, when the door opened in front of her and Connor swung out. He had an aluminium crutch under each arm and, beneath the leg of his jeans, a white gauze-covered plaster pointed his left foot down at an angle.

'Hop-along Malone,' he said drily.

'Or Rudolf Nureyev.' She shone him a mischievous smile. 'Maybe you should buy a pair of ballet tights?'

'Maybe you should drive me home,' he responded.

During their time at the hospital, darkness had fallen and the rush-hour traffic had dwindled. Following directions, Jennet drove around the huge circle of Hammersmith Broadway and cut off beneath a flyover into a maze of narrower residential streets. She turned into a quiet road which ran beside the Thames.

On one side stood houses—old and new, stone and brick, some grandly porched, some cottagey and bearded with wisteria. On the other side, shadowy gardens sloped gracefully down to a river which glistened like black satin in the moonlight.

'We're in luck,' Connor said. 'See the tall white house? That's where I have my apartment. And see the empty space between the cars immediately outside? That's where you can park.'

'You live on the third floor,' she said, when he had levered himself out of the Fiesta and onto his crutches. 'Is there a lift or do you have to hop up the stairs?'

'Hop, unfortunately, but I'll manage.'

'I'll come up behind to catch you if you should fall,' she told him.

He gave a dry smile. 'If I fall, chances are I'll send you flying too. But thanks.'

The carpeted stairs were steep. Lifting himself up from one step to the next demanded a continuous effort and by the time he reached the first landing his forehead was glazed with perspiration.

'You could try the next flight sitting down,' she suggested, when he stopped to rest.

Connor nodded, but after shifting himself up a few steps on his backside he decided that progress was easier on the crutches.

'I'll need to allow myself plenty of time to get down in the morning,' he said, leaning against the bannister as he caught his breath at the second floor.

'You're not intending to go to work tomorrow?' Jennet protested.

'Yes.'

'But the consultant said to rest your leg—and going downstairs will be far more hazardous than coming up—and—' She broke off as other aspects of his disability hit her. 'Is there someone who can watch out for you when you're on the stairs, and shop and cook et cetera. A girlfriend—or a partner?' she added, suddenly realising that he might not live alone.

The grapevine had not reported any current attachment, but the grapevine would not know everything.

'I have neither a partner nor a girlfriend.'

'No?' she said doubtfully.

'No,' Connor rapped. 'If you check the gossip which you seem to have been hearing, you'll find that my playboy reputation is several years out of date. I don't deny that at one time I did follow my basic—or baser—instincts and played the field, but I've changed. I've learned sense and about time because I'm damn near forty. And,' he said, starting to heave himself doggedly up the final flight of stairs, 'right now I feel like it.'

His journey was laboured. There were a couple of times when he stopped and needed to visibly gather up his strength in order to continue. And when he reached the top floor they both heaved a sigh of relief.

Connor unlocked the white-glossed door and stretched a hand inside to switch on lights.

'After you,' he said.

Jennet walked into a spacious cream-carpeted living room with a dining area at the far end. Green and cream striped curtains framed two large windows which overlooked the river and gave a view of sparkling lights in the darkness of the far bank. A vast rubber plant grew in a corner. The furniture was a mix of modern teak, antique rosewood and items such as a battered brass-bound chest, which looked as if he had picked them up cheap at an auction. Yet the pieces fitted together as though they were meant for each other.

A collection of photographs, water colours and sketches were pinned to one wall, while bookshelves filled another. Some books had escaped from the shelves and lay around on chairs and on the carpet, as did the occasional shirt, discarded newspapers, and, oddly, a child's wooden rocking horse which had lost its ears and had a moth-eaten raffia mane and tail.

Connor hopped across to a dark green leather sofa, propped his crutches against an adjacent armchair and slumped down. He looked exhausted.

'Is there a neighbour who could help you?' she asked.

He shook his head. 'The apartment below is empty, the woman from the first floor has gone to Australia to see her new grandson and the young couple at ground level are social types who always seem to be out. But I'll be fine. Thanks for bringing me home—'

'I'm not leaving yet,' Jennet declared. 'You need to eat.'

'I can make myself a sandwich. I have cheese,' he said, thinking, 'and there's some left-over sausage and—'

'Cheese and cold sausage?' she protested. 'Do you know what a sandwich like that will do for your digestion?'

'No,' he said impatiently, 'but I'm afraid you're going to tell me.'

'It'll guarantee a sleepless night and this is one night when you need to sleep. Do you have any eggs?' He nodded. 'And do you like cheese omelette?'

'Yes.'

'I shall make you one. It's the least I can do,' she said, when he started to protest.

'You're trying to redeem yourself?'

'That's the general idea—and,' she added, 'as the saying goes, the way to every man's heart is through his stomach.'

'Aren't you aiming a little high?' Connor asked drily. 'But I am hungry. You'll join me? By the time you get home it's going to be late to start on dinner,' he pointed out.

'I'll join you,' she agreed.

He gestured through an archway to a compact arrangement of light oak cupboards and white worktops. 'There's the kitchen and the eggs are in the fridge.'

'And the cheese? And a whisk? And plates?'

He told her where to find the various ingredients and utensils, and as the omelette cooked she set the table. Coffee was perked and ice cream taken from the freezer. In a surprisingly short time, they were eating.

'My answering machine's flashing,' he said, suddenly noticing as he drank his coffee. 'Someone's probably called from the studios; would you play it for me?'

Walking over to the telephone which sat on a rosewood desk, Jennet pushed the switch.

'Hi, Dad,' a voice said, 'it's your son and heir.'

Her head whipped round and she stared at him. 'Dad?' she queried as it flashed through her mind that the call must be a wrong number.

'That's right,' he said, and raised a long finger to his lips. 'Hush.'

'Just to let you know that I've reached Cordes, which is a medieval hill town towards the bottom of France,' the voice went on. 'Everything's going real well and I've yet to be set upon by Rottweilers or held at gunpoint by Middle Eastern suicide bombers. So you can untwist your knickers, right? I've met these two Danish guys who are also doing Europe and we're going to travel on to Nice together and plan to take a spin around Monte Carlo. I'll try and catch you sometime tomorrow. Love you, Russ.'

The machine fell silent.

'You have a son?' she said, crossing to sit down again at the table.

The fact that Connor was a father put him in an entirely different light.

'I do.' His gaze was cool and steady. 'You're not the only one who's a privacy freak. Lester knows about Russ, as do one or two others at the studios, but I prefer to keep my personal life to myself.' Irritation darkened his eyes. 'Which hasn't always been possible.

'It was Russ who liked the spaghetti hoop advert,' he told her. 'He used to sing your song ad nauseam, which is why I remember it.'

'How old is he?' Jennet asked.

'Coming up to nineteen. He finished school last summer and is having a year out before going on to college.'

'You must've been married very young.'

'I was twenty-one, which—and I realise this is rent-a-cliché—is far too young. I divorced young, too,' he said, and his face took on a shuttered look.

She eyed the rocking horse. 'Do you have any more children?'

'No, just Russ.' He noticed the direction of her gaze. 'I'm mending that for—' there was a split-second hesitation '—the daughter of a friend. Russ and I have always gone on holiday together,' he said, 'but this year he decided he wanted to spend time hiking around Europe on his own. Or, at least, without his old man. Which is understandable at his age.'

'Would you have wanted to go hiking?' she enquired.

Connor grimaced. 'No way. My idea of a holiday is to lie around in the sun with a good book and a gin and tonic close by.' He raked back his hair with a weary hand. 'Lying down is beginning to seem like a good idea right now.'

'I'll wash up and then I'll go,' she said, rising to start clearing the table. 'But I'll be back in the morning to see you down the stairs at—what—nine o'clock?'

'You'll drive all the way home, grab a few hours' sleep, and drive all the way back here?' He shook his head. 'No. I appreciate your offer, but I can get one of the Ensign drivers to collect me tomorrow and stand guard as I descend.'

'Fine,' Jennet agreed, bending to lift a couple of books from the floor and return them to the shelves.

'There's no need for you to start tidying up,' Connor said curtly, as if advising that this was *his* territory and he resented her interference. 'I may not be genetically disposed towards housework, but I happen to like a bit of clutter. When it gets to be knee-high I shall remove it, but until then—'

'Until then you'll have no space in which to swing your crutches and be forever in danger of tripping over something?' she said.

He considered this. 'Point taken. Go ahead.'

'Does your son live with you?' she asked as she collected other books and put them away.

She saw that his piece of lead crystal was sitting on the shelves. The glass tiger had been splintered, Jennet thought. Momentarily.

'No, he lives with his mother though he spends a lot of time here,' he said, locking his crutches beneath his armpits and starting to help her. 'I've always lived alone.'

'You haven't...cohabited since your divorce?'

'Never.' Connor looked around. 'All done. I'll help you with the pots,' he said, trapezing towards her.

'Don't bother.'

'It's no bother. I—'

He was alongside the sofa when the rubber tip of one crutch landed on the corner of a glossy magazine which was peeping out and which neither of them had noticed, skidded and went flying.

As he started to topple sideways, Jennet leapt forward. She rushed at him, pushing at his shoulders to keep him upright. He half twisted, made a wild grab and together they fell down onto the dark green leather. There was a soft thud. And silence.

'Is your leg all right?' she gasped.

She was lying half beneath him, pressed against his chest. She could feel the weight of his body and the pounding of his heart—a frantic pounding which seemed to echo her own.

Connor rolled from her. 'It's survived. How about you?'

'I've survived too,' she said, sitting up.

His dark brows drew together. 'I don't think I will go into work tomorrow,' he said. 'And it's going to be tricky getting around the studios.'

'An obstacle course,' Jennet declared. She paused. She was responsible for his accident. It was her fault that he had landed up on crutches. 'Lester suggested you should come with me to Capri,' she said slowly. 'You're going to find life restrictive here, so why not join me for three weeks?'

Connor looked at her. He was silent for so long that she began to wonder if he would ever speak, then he nodded.

'OK,' he said.

CHAPTER FIVE

THE scooter bounced along one side of the tiny piazza, passing an ancient parish church, hole-in-the-wall *gelaterias*, cafés where tourists sat idly chatting and sipping cappuccino at outside tables. A cut along a *via*, one of the cobbled alleyways which were lined with boutiques selling chic Italian designer fashions, a swerve past boxed orange trees demarcating the portalled entrance to a jet-set hotel, and Capri town was behind them.

Her hands firm on the handlebars, Jennet gazed across tranquil fields of wild flowers, down through vineyards and olive trees, to the grey-blue Mediterranean which lay far below. Gigantic rocks speared up out of the water. Seagulls soared. A lone fishing boat chugged around the dramatically plunging coast.

Lifting her eyes to the sky, she sighed. Ever since they had arrived four days ago—flying into Naples and taking the ferry from Sorrento to Capri's Marina Grande—a blanket of cloud had hung over the island and there had been intermittent showers. The temperature was warm, in the seventies, but she wanted clear skies and sunshine. She wanted her guest to see Capri in all its beauty.

'You're not wearing your wedding ring,' Connor remarked, all of a sudden.

He was sitting behind her on the scooter, holding onto her around the waist and with his plaster-casted leg propped up on the foot-rest. His crutches were held upright in the loop of his other arm.

'I left it at home.' She glanced down at her bare left hand. 'I didn't want people to think we were married.'

He made no comment and a beat or two of silence went by. 'Did you and your husband have a special reason for buying a villa here?' he enquired.

'We didn't buy it,' Jennet said. 'My stepfather gave me the house.'

'Freddie gives houses as well as dressing gowns?'

'No, the stepfather in question was Tommaso, an Italian businessman. When I stayed at the villa with him and my mother I fell in love with Capri, and when they split he signed it over to me.'

'Now that's what I call generosity!'

'It was generous and very kind, though Tommaso is wealthy and owns property all over the place. Even if we could've afforded to buy a house here, which we couldn't, Stuart would never've done anything so wild,' she went on.

'Wild?'

'He would've regarded buying a property in Italy as wild. Wild as in risky,' she defined. She was looking ahead and sending her words back over her shoulder. 'Could he trust the foreign lawyers? Did the rents represent a good return on capital? If you only went a couple of times a year were you making the wisest use of the money? Stuart didn't think so and he was keen for me to sell, but I refused. He wasn't—'

'Watch out!' Connor yelped as a moped carrying two earnestly gossiping youths shot out around the corner of a house a few yards ahead of them.

'No danger,' she assured him, and frowned.

The interruption had come at just the right time because she had been criticising Stuart—more or less.

'I'm not sure that fixing this scooter was such a bright idea, after all,' he said grimly, when she accelerated and darted past the youths with inches to spare.

'It was a great idea,' she tossed back. 'And there's no need to panic—I have driven it before.'

'Yes, years ago, and then you appear to have taken lessons from a racing driver,' he said, his voice dry in her ear. 'Which is why, although I arrived with just a few silver hairs, I could go back completely white.'

When Tommaso had given her the villa, which he had rarely visited, he had given it complete with contents. In the cellar amongst mounds of jumble, she had discovered the scooter. It had not functioned—until Connor had spent an afternoon tinkering with the engine, fiddling with the plug and oiling it.

Jennet glanced down at the panniers. Now she was able to transport the shopping with ease and speed. Or, at least, the journey would have been easy if she had not been forever aware of the man riding shotgun behind, his arm around her waist, his chest at her back, his legs parallel with her legs. He might appear to be clinging on for dear life at times, but to her the closeness was erotic.

A line etched itself between her brows. She wished Connor were at ease, but since meeting her at the airport he had been a touch formal and far too tense.

On first noticing his tension, she had decided that his leg must be troubling him, but whenever she asked he assured her he was not in any pain. Admittedly, he could be making the claim falsely to stop her from feeling guilty, yet he showed no visible sign of suffering and was becoming astonishingly adept on his crutches.

So she had turned over a second possibility in her mind. Could his tension spring from an unease at being

alone with her? She had recalled his statement about
how he had 'learned sense' and stopped playing the romantic field. Had he stopped because he had finally
realised that no other woman could ever take the place
of his wife—for whom he still hankered? Did his aversion
to live-in relationships demonstrate a respect for the
woman's memory and the sanctity of their marriage?
And might Connor feel that in accepting the invitation
to come and stay with her in Capri—albeit briefly and
platonically—he was somehow being disloyal?

Jennet's frown deepened. She had felt almost obliged
to invite him, but instead of waiting what had seemed
like hours for his reply she should have smartly told him
to forget it. She had not had the sense, and now she was
saddled with a brooding and obviously reluctant guest.

She bumped off the end of the metalled road and onto
an unmade lane. Their living together had given rise to
a tension inside her, too, though for a different reason.
Ironically, she found the day-to-day domestic situation
seductive. It did not matter that Connor was edgy; being
one half of a couple had reminded her of the basic
pleasure of having someone to talk to, someone to share
meals with, how comforting it felt to know there was
someone else in the house when she went to bed at night.
Being with him had emphasised the disadvantages of
going solo.

Yet his male presence was double-edged. Whilst the
awareness of him lying downstairs 'between the sheets'
might make her feel good from a security angle, it inspired all kinds of unfortunate thoughts which pro-
hibited sleep. She moistened her lips. She had found
herself wondering what he wore in bed or whether, like
her, he did not wear anything. She had imagined him—

'The front shutters are finished,' Connor said.

They were approaching the pink-walled and red-roofed villa which stood at the end of the lane. It was within shouting distance of a couple of other dwellings, but circling thickets of leafy trees afforded a pleasant privacy.

Jennet grinned. Before the wooden shutters had been a peeling brown, but now they shone a glossy fir-green.

'They look good, too.'

When she stopped the scooter beside pots of scarlet bougainvillea which edged the tiled frontage to the house, he lifted himself off and onto his crutches.

'My gluteus maximus is going to need time to recover from all that bouncing around,' he declared, stretching back a hand to rub at his backside.

She gave a taut smile. Like her, Connor was wearing shirt and shorts. His shorts were a brief pair of khaki cotton which fitted neatly. She had noticed, in her wing mirror, both local women and female tourists admiringly eyeing him—and his gluteus maximus—as he had travelled behind her.

She was unfastening the panniers when the elder of the two workmen, a silver-haired charmer with a bushy moustache, appeared from the back of the house. He carried a tool bag and had shed his overalls to reveal a smart striped shirt and dark trousers. Like most of his countrymen, he was a snappy dresser.

'All shutters in place,' he announced.

Although she had picked up some Italian it was limited, so the man spoke in fractured and heavily accented English. And, being a Latin male, he demonstrated an irritating tendency to direct his words to Connor, the perceived boss, rather than towards her.

'Tomorrow we fix tiles on balcony,' he continued, wafting his arms around in descriptive gestures. 'OK, *signore*?'

'Yes, thank you,' Jennet said firmly.

'*Signore?*' the workman asked.

Connor cast her an amused look. 'OK,' he replied.

'He's the type who believes women belong either in the kitchen or in the bedroom,' she said, as the man joined his companion who was already waiting in their van.

'The sensible type?' he said, deadpan.

She slitted her eyes at him. 'If you were not on crutches...' she threatened, and hauled out a bag and marched inside.

'Speaking of women in bedrooms, would you like to give me a hand moving the beds in the spare room, so that I can get busy painting first thing in the morning?' he said, when the shopping had been unpacked.

He had insisted on helping to carry in the bags. He might be a reluctant guest and injured, but he was a courteous one. He had also shown a pleasing interest in the house—an interest which translated into the practical.

'I thought you liked to spend your holidays lying around with a good book and a gin and tonic?' she said.

'I will do, once the sun comes out.'

Jennet gave him a wry look. 'I bet.'

When she had toured the villa to discover the extent of the damage, Connor had accompanied her. Six pairs of shutters had been smashed together with corresponding windows, and floor tiles on the balcony of her bedroom were shattered. After helping to brush up broken glass and clean, he had suggested that he should repaint the spare bedroom, which, admittedly, was shabby.

'I need something to do while you're writing,' he had said, when she had protested, so this afternoon they had brought back brushes and a couple of cans of apricot-white emulsion.

They now made their way to the spare room, which, like her room, was upstairs at the back of the house and looked out over fields towards the ocean, contained three single old-fashioned iron beds, a large walnut chest of drawers and wardrobe, bedside tables and chairs.

'Push,' Connor encouraged.

She pressed hard with both hands and her full weight. 'I—am—pushing,' she panted.

'Harder.'

'I'm—doing—my best, but I'm not a Neanderthal like you and it seems—to be stuck.'

They were moving the huge wardrobe towards the middle of the room where everything else had been gathered.

'Let me,' he instructed, and, abandoning his crutches, he hopped on one leg, heaved with a muscled shoulder and manoeuvred the wardrobe into place with insulting ease.

'A week makes a big difference,' Jennet observed wryly.

Connor frowned. 'Sorry?'

'Seven days back you found it a real struggle making it up the stairs, but now you can damn near dance the fandango—with or without your crutches,' she said, thinking that had he stayed home and practised a little he would have been whizzing around the studios.

'I don't like to be beaten by anything or—' he cast her a look '—by anyone. Next we take down the curtains.'

'Yes, boss,' she said, her sassy reply tinged with resentment. Whilst she appreciated his willingness to help, she would have appreciated it more if he could have re-laxed and *enjoyed* her company.

Jennet had commandeered a chair, climbed up and was unhooking a curtain when a thought suddenly came into her head.

'The day I called at your office to tell you about my Beth/Dinsdale idea, you said you needed to talk to me,' she remembered. 'What was it you wanted to talk about?'

'I was going to tell you to quit your bitching and get writing a toyboy romance, or else.'

'Or else what?' she queried, glancing back at where Connor balanced on his crutches.

'Or else I'd need to think about bringing in another writer to work alongside and get them to do it.'

Shock and outrage swung her around. She would have fallen off the chair if she had not grabbed hold of the second curtain, which remained *in situ*.

'Another writer!' she protested.

'Plenty of series are joint efforts and—' determi-nation added a stony slant to his jaw '—I'm not pre-pared to stand by and allow *Hutton's Spa* to fail.'

'You reckon if there isn't love interest that might happen?'

'It shouldn't with the next series because there's always a roll-on effect, but thereafter viewers might start to lose interest and ratings could slip. And, as you're aware, Ensign does regard it as long-term. OK, you would've cut up rough,' he continued, 'but—'

'I'd have pulled out,' Jennet declared.

Connor fixed her with narrowed grey eyes. 'You would've abandoned *Hutton's Spa* and said goodbye to all the money you could've earned?'

'Yes!'

'Just because an affair between a younger man and
an older woman offends you? Though it beats me why
you should be so damn paranoid.' He shook his head.
'You wouldn't have done it.'

'I would! You wouldn't really have brought in another
writer and let me pull out—would you?' she said, her
question treading a precarious line between a plea and
an indignant protest.

'If it'd come to the crunch. Though first I'd have tried
some other way to persuade you to see sense,' he added.

'Like what?' Jennet asked.

'Can't say.' His eyes travelled from her face, over the
lines of her body and down the length of her bare legs.
'But I'd have thought of something. However, the situation hasn't arisen.'

Not yet, she thought. Connor might have agreed to
consider the draft which she had begun to work on, but
there was no guarantee of approval. And if he did not
approve he would return to his earlier demand.

As she started to unhook the second curtain, she
frowned. His look had seemed to imply that he might
have attempted to persuade her to do his bidding by
making love to her. Would he have used such a tactic?
Would she have *allowed* him to use it, even though it
was destined to fail in its purpose? She would like to
think that she was neither so dumb nor so pliable, and
yet—

Jumping down from the chair, she gathered up the
two curtains. 'I'll put these in the washing machine and
get busy on dinner,' she said.

'Could you shampoo my hair?' Connor asked, appearing in the doorway of the kitchen quarter of an
hour later.

Jennet turned to look at him. His shorts had been exchanged for pale cotton chinos and he was bare-chested. A damp sheen to his skin and his clean-razored jaw indicated that he had just washed and shaved. There was a tantalising whiff of men's cologne.

She pasted on a smile. 'Sure,' she said.

The downstairs bedroom came with its own blue and white tiled bathroom, which included a bath with a hand-held shower. Bathing with his plastered leg hanging over the side and showering in the upstairs shower cubicle with it stuck out of the door or wrapped in polythene had proved to be uncomfortable and unsatisfactory. So for the past couple of days he had given himself stand-up all-over washes, and she had followed on and washed his hair.

As she went with him into the bathroom, her heartbeat broke into a gallop. When he had first asked for as-sistance, she had immediately agreed. But to rub in the shampoo, to rinse and towel dry—to be actively *grooming* the man—were intimate actions.

Connor stood on his good leg, rested his other knee on the side of the bath and leant forward.

'No call from Russ,' he said as she wet his head and applied shampoo.

Jennet blinked. She had been mesmerised by the smooth, pale honey stretch of his long back, by the width of his shoulders, by the roll of bunched muscles in his upper arms.

'Sorry?'

'I gave him this number in case he wanted to get in touch, but he hasn't rung yet.'

Holding the shower in one hand and ruffling his hair with the other, she rinsed away foam. 'What you mean is *you* want him to get in touch,' she said.

'Correct. When he was small there were a couple of years when I didn't see him and ever since I've needed to keep a frequent check and to know that he's safe.' She saw a frown furrow the side of his brow. 'I feel so guilty about those years.'

'Does your son blame you for not seeing him? Does he consider he missed out?' she enquired.

'He's never said anything to me.'

'And you've never asked him?'

'No.'

'But you're a pretty blunt, up-front kind of a person,' Jennet protested.

'Maybe, but maybe I prefer not to hear him condemn me,' he said, and moved his shoulders in an uncharac-teristic gesture of defeat.

'Why didn't you see him?' she asked as she squeezed a dollop of banana conditioner from a plastic bottle and started to massage it into the dark strands.

His hair was thick and vital. Worn a touch too long to be fashionable, it curled around his ears and came to a neat, arrowing point in the nape of his neck. It was the kind of point which called out to be stroked, she thought—or kissed, even if you did end up with a mouthful of bubbles.

'Because I left my wife and went to work in the States—and once I'd left it was difficult to go back, from the distance point of view, financially and emotionally, because my marriage was under stress.' His voice became gritty. 'I was such a bastard.'

'We all do things we regret,' she said, 'and you can't have been exactly mature at the time.'

'In my early twenties, so I wasn't too great on either patience or understanding. That feels nice,' Connor said suddenly.

'Having your head massaged?'

'No, the rub of your breast against my shoulder,' he said and frowned, as though the observation had unfortunately slipped out.

'When Russ rings, if he'd like to come and stay for a few days he's very welcome,' she told him, sluicing off the conditioner and now making sure that she stood well clear. 'There're beds to spare.'

'Thanks. Capri isn't on his itinerary, but I'll mention it.'

She dried his hair and passed him the towel to dry his face. 'All finished.'

'You're very kind,' he said.

Jennet gave a silent groan. He had been talking and sharing his troubles, which had seemed like progress, but his awareness of the brush of her body—and his comment—had knocked him back into being formal again. It had also revived her tension.

'Just part of the service,' she replied as he pulled on a yellow sports shirt. 'How's about we have a glass of wine before dinner?'

Connor combed his dark hair back from his brow. 'Sounds good,' he agreed.

In the kitchen, she opened a bottle of Frascati and put it with two glasses onto a tray. Dinner was to be the mozzarella and aubergine pizza which they had bought at a delicatessen, served with a green salad, so preparations would not take long.

When she carried the tray out onto the terrace which stretched across the rear of the house, her guest was seated in a rattan armchair, with his leg resting on a footstool. The two chairs, stool, plus a sofa and a basket chair which was suspended from an upstairs balcony, were all fitted with fat cushions covered in a poppiesin-cornfield print. Pots of trailing purple pelargoniums, which miraculously survived from one visit to the next, lightened one corner, while periwinkles nodded white faces in another.

The sky made a ceiling of grey and a breeze had sprung up, stirring oleander bushes which grew in the small back garden and rattling nearby palms. A smell of rain hung in the evening air.

'Would you be interested in a series—say a six-parter—about a small private airline and its owner who fights to save it from being gobbled up by an international conglomerate?' Jennet asked, as she poured their drinks. 'It's only an idea and obviously I couldn't do it while *Hutton's Spa* is taking up so much of my time, but I wondered.'

'I'd be very interested—and I'd be interested in any other ideas you may have. If you'd like to sketch out a treatment I'll show it to Lester.'

'Thanks. I will do.'

'Has someone been telling you tales of how they fought to save an airline?' Connor enquired as she sat down.

She nodded. 'Someone did, though not a stepfather. At least, not an official one.'

'How many stepfathers have you had?' he asked curiously.

'Just two. After my father died, when I was twelve, my mother married Freddie, who lasted from my being around thirteen to sixteen. Tommaso appeared on the scene when I was twenty and exited four years later. But in between the stepfathers my mother had other... relationships. One of them was with a guy who ran his own airline, was pounced on by a major league player, but survived.'

'Your mother sounds to have been an active lady where menfriends are concerned,' Connor remarked.

'She still is,' she said wryly, and paused.

Should she reveal her parentage? she wondered, feeling abruptly tempted to forgo discretion and come clean. But if she did she would be faced with the usual round of interminable questions. She sipped at her wine. She would also stop being Jennet Galbraith, the writer, in his mind and take on a different, additional—and not altogether welcome—persona.

'You appear to be as anchored as the *Cutty Sark*,' he said, shifting his leg into a more comfortable position on the footstool. 'But didn't you find her...gallivanting, as Lester'd call it, hard to take?'

'Not really, because I was prepared for it. My father had cancer and knew he was dying, and in his final weeks he talked to me about the future,' she explained. 'He warned me that unless my mother found another strong individual like himself she could go haywire. He said she'd have constant boyfriends and maybe would marry again, but that I mustn't be distressed. He said she needed to be admired and needed excitement, that it was part of her character, but she also needed me.'

'Because you were strong, like him?'

'I guess.'

'No guessing. You are strong—and can be a stubborn little filly,' he said drily.

Jennet stuck out her tongue.

'And juvenile, at times,' he added.

'My mother has an aptitude for attracting men who are emotional cripples and who couldn't make a commitment to a boiled egg,' she went on. 'They've all been lightweight characters. Great fun and friendly, but blasé, lackadaisical and not too fussed when things ended.'

'Your mother hasn't been too fussed, either?'

'No. She sails along through life, always carefree, always pleasant. Her divorces have been amicable and she and I both keep in touch with her ex-husbands. She's also beautiful, which plays a part, and has charm by the bucketload.' A shadow flickered across her face. 'If you met her, you'd fall for her. Most men do.'

'The constant uncertainty of not knowing how long a relationship would last must've affected you,' he said.

She hesitated. People were usually so dazzled by what they saw as the *glamour* of her mother's lifestyle that they never looked beyond her bland assurances, but Connor was more perceptive. His tone had also sounded compassionate, which encouraged her to talk.

'I wasn't conscious of it at the time, but in retrospect, yes,' she said slowly. 'Remember I told you I was always writing when I was a teenager? I used to write stories about families with mothers who were mumsy and ultra-reliable.' Her lips curved. 'They wore pinnies and baked cakes, and were forever taking their children around museums.'

'Which your mother didn't do?'

'Never, though I'm not complaining. Whatever I missed in those directions, I gained in others. She took me with her to different countries, like Italy, and we seemed to be forever moving house, going places, meeting people. There was never a dull moment.' She became grave. 'But I think writing was a form of therapy. Though I'd had twelve years of my father's steadying influence, so I'd had a good start.'

'Did your mother have an eye for the men when they were married?' Connor enquired.

She gave a rueful nod. 'Yes, she's a great flirt. But she loved him and respected him and she never cheated.

He always kept a sense of humour about her behaviour, made allowances and was accepting. I'm accepting, too.'

His brow furrowed. He looked as if he was about to make a comment, but then he held out his hand.

'It's raining,' he said. 'Time to go indoors.'

Jennet struggled up through the drugged haze of sleep. There was a noise. An intermittent drip...drip...drip on wooden floorboards. Rubbing her eyes, she rolled over onto her back. She jerked up. Ugh, there was a cold wet patch at one side of the bed. She fumbled for the switch on the bedside light.

'Oh, no,' she complained, blinking.

The rain which had started early evening and now beat against the shutters in a muffled thrum was the heaviest there had been since they had arrived. When the storm had hit the previous week, it must have also dislodged roof tiles for water was dripping onto her bed, making a small puddle in front of the dressing table and plopping spasmodically down from the ceiling beside the window.

Staggering up, she pushed her bed out from under the fall of the drip and went through to the landing linen cupboard to find towels. They were sited to soak up the wet. Next came a whistle-stop tour of the upper floor, but she found no more leaks. Thank goodness.

What did she do now? she wondered. Where should she go? She could not sleep on a damp mattress and extracting one of the iron beds from the piled-up furniture in the spare room was beyond her. She retrieved the white blanket which she had kicked down and which remained dry. She would sleep on the sofa in the living room.

Pulling on the dusky pink shortie nightgown which she kept as a stand-by, Jennet made her way quietly downstairs. A table lamp was lit. Cushions were placed at one end of the gold brocade sofa and the blanket arranged. She wrinkled her nose. All sleepy feeling had gone. She was hungry. She would find something to eat.

Padding barefoot across the cream ceramic floor, she went into the kitchen. She was peering into the fridge wondering what to choose—fruit? Cheese? A carrot?—when the door creaked. She looked back over her shoulder, to find Connor standing on his crutches. His dark hair was dishevelled over his brow. His feet were bare. All he wore was a pair of white boxer shorts.

'Hello,' she said, a little breathlessly.

His hands tightened around the holding bars of his sticks. He had decided that the lamp in the living room must have been left on by mistake and the kitchen light, too. He had not expected Jennet to be downstairs. Downstairs in a short nightdress which clung to her body like a second skin and bent half double, as if offering the rounded curves of her backside to him.

A nerve pulsed in his temple. He had been thinking of her lying in bed in her room and to be faced with her so scantily clad and looking so desirable seemed like a dirty trick. An affront. He shifted his stance. It was also instant arousal.

'What the hell are you doing here?' he demanded.

She straightened up and faced him. He looked moody and cross.

'What am *I* doing here? You're a real cutie-pie,' she snapped. 'I'm finding something to eat—in the kitchen of my own house. And if that's thrown you into one of those tantrums which the doctor warned me about I have just one thing to say—go wiggle your toes!'

She was not sure why she was snapping and felt so irritated by his presence. Perhaps it was because he had startled her, or because she had picked up on his annoyance, or because her resentment at him being such a reluctant guest was finally bubbling over.

'I am not having a tantrum,' he said heavily.

'But you are wandering around in the middle of the night. Why?' she enquired.

'I came to get a drink of water.'

'Did I wake you?'

'No, I wasn't asleep,' he replied, his tone terse. 'You couldn't sleep either?'

'On the contrary, I was fast asleep.' Jennet hooked up the shoestring strap of her nightgown which had slipped down over one shoulder. 'But I woke up because it's raining in through the roof.'

Connor muttered an oath. 'How bad is it?'

'Not too serious, but my bed's wet and so I decided that rather than attempt to dismantle the mountain of furniture in the spare room I'd sleep down here.'

'Down here?' he said sharply.

'Don't worry, I have no intention of turfing you out of your bed. I shall be sleeping on the sofa. Sorry if that displeases you,' she said, when he frowned, 'but tough! And while we're on the subject of displeasure,' she continued, the momentum of her irritation keeping her going, 'there's nothing to stop you from curtailing your stay here and getting on the next plane.'

He stood straighter. 'You want me to leave?'

'I think it's more a case of *you* wanting to leave,' she retorted.

'Me?'

'I realise you regret your decision to come to Capri, but if you have a hang-up about your wife that is not my fault,' Jennet said tartly. 'I believe there are daily flights from Naples so tomorrow why not—?'

'A hang-up about my wife?' he broke in.

'You...hanker after her. She still means something to you.'

Connor repositioned his crutches. 'What are you talking about?'

'Earlier today you told me how you felt such a bastard about leaving to work in the States and how difficult it was to go back. But I assume you wish you had gone back—that you'd never been divorced.'

'God, no! I shall have to sit down,' he said, turning and hop-swinging into the living room. 'This standing up business is killing me.'

Jennet followed him. 'So it's your leg which is the problem,' she said as he lowered himself down into one of the brocade armchairs. 'Why have you continually insisted that it's fine when—?'

'It *is* fine. I get tired when I'm standing up and—' he shot a look at the clock on the mantelpiece '—especially when it's two o'clock in the morning, but that's all. I went to the States because it felt as if my wife—my ex-wife—was suffocating me, and whilst I feel bad about leaving Russ I don't regret parting from her. You wouldn't like to get me that drink of water?' he appealed. 'And then I'll explain.'

She filled a glass with sparkling water and found herself an apple. Returning, she sat on the sofa, tucked up her knees and wrapped the blanket around her. It was not cold, but the repeated flicker of her companion's gaze had made her aware of how her nightdress clung and revealed. Her teeth bit through the skin of the apple. She was also alarmingly aware of his bedroomy look and bare torso.

'You don't want to put something on?' she suggested, eyeing the hair which started above his navel and grew onwards and upwards like dark ivy.

Connor shook his head. 'I'm hot-blooded. Back to basics,' he said, starting his tale. 'The only reason Polly and I got married was because she was pregnant. We both got carried away one night and that was that.'

'How old was your wife?'

'Nineteen.'

'She didn't consider having an abortion?' Jennet enquired. 'I wouldn't, but—'

'She didn't and neither did I. I was determined our child would be born and determined to accept my responsibilities.' He took a mouthful of water. 'When our folks voiced doubts about whether rushing into marriage was wise and whether it'd last, I insisted that it would. I refused to accept the evidence and all the statistics which show that the younger people marry, the greater the likelihood of divorce.' He gave a humourless smile. 'At twenty-one you think you know everything.'

'How long had you known each other before she became pregnant?'

'Three months. We'd rubbed along fine as boyfriend and girlfriend, but the moment we set up house together it became blindingly apparent that we weren't compatible. Polly may've been training to become a pharmacist, but her true aim—her only aim—was to be a housewife and mother.'

'At nineteen?' Jennet protested.

'At nineteen. She didn't understand how I could be fired with ambition and eager to get started on my career.'

'You were still studying when you married?'

'Yes, though I also worked every spare hour in a hamburger joint in order to help keep us. Both sets of parents assisted, thank the Lord,' Connor said, 'though it wasn't easy for them. However, I kept a tally of the hand-outs which we received and, in time, I paid it all back. When Russ was born, Polly was in seventh heaven,' he continued. 'Within weeks she was saying that we must have another baby, soon because she didn't want much of a gap between them.'

She shook a wondering head. 'Nuts.'

'That was my reaction. I pointed out that we couldn't support one child, let alone two, plus I suggested that we needed to establish ourselves as a couple before we considered enlarging our family, but she wouldn't be dissuaded. Over the next couple of years I made damn sure she didn't become pregnant again—which is what I should've done in the first place,' he said brusquely, 'but Polly never let the subject drop. When I started to work in television—as a lowly researcher—she increased the pressure.'

'She reckoned it was a green light for a second baby then?'

'She did, but I didn't. She started to nag, not just about wanting another child, but also complained if I worked late or left things around the house or if I didn't get Russ to put his toys away the minute he'd finished playing with them.' Connor groaned. 'She was so house-proud.'

'This is why you were sniffy about me tidying away the books at your apartment?' she enquired.

He nodded. 'Polly had to have everything so damn neat and tidy and, for a moment, it seemed like you were the same.' He took another swig of water. 'Her nagging became so incessant that I used to dread walking in through the front door, yet I hung on.' His expression was grim. 'I was unhappy, she was unhappy. I recognised that our marriage had been ill-fated from the start, but I hated the idea of divorce.'

'Because everyone would say "We told you so"?'

'That, but also because I believe in old-fashioned family values—settled marriages, doing your best for your kids, no adultery. Then the company which I worked for offered me a job with an associated station in New York. Polly suggested I should go and I was straight out the door. I was so desperate to get away that there was no soul-searching and no thought about the effect my absence might have on Russ. When it dawned on me and I came back, Polly said she wanted a divorce.'

Jennet chewed at the apple. 'Would you have asked her for one?'

'Yes, I had my speech all ready. I hadn't committed adultery,' he went on. 'It was four years from my leaving for the States to the divorce becoming final, but during that time I was the soul of virtue. I don't know why I'm dumping my life history on you,' he said, all of a sudden. 'I'm not usually into true confessions.'

'Perhaps you needed to talk?' she suggested.

'Perhaps. Or perhaps, like your stepfathers *et al*, I just find it easy to talk to you,' Connor said pensively. 'Because I'd been married at twenty-one, the romances which I had after the divorce were only like the romances which most men go through before they embark on matrimony,' he continued. 'I was making up for lost time.'

'Because you'd had four years of self-imposed virtue,' Jennet said. 'It was understandable.'

'Maybe. However, because I felt I'd been trapped into marriage, I was determined I wouldn't be trapped again. So I always made it clear that meaningful relationships were not on the agenda and I wasn't husband material.'

'The fear of being trapped is why you've never lived with anyone?'

'No.'

Her brow creased. 'It isn't?'

'I've never lived with anyone because I didn't want to set a bad example for my son.' He put his empty glass aside. 'I realise how crazy that sounds, but Russ never met any of the women whom I—'

'Dated?' she provided, when he paused.

His lips moved in a wry curve. 'Right. And as long as I lived alone there was no need for him to meet them. OK, as he grew older he must've realised his father didn't live like a monk, but he never had to confront any evidence. Gossip always exaggerates and whilst I did have affairs I did not have *so* many,' Connor said, and starfished a hand on his bare chest. 'We're not talking a sexual cowboy here.'

'I believe you,' Jennet told him.

'Truly?'

'Truly.'

He grinned. 'Thanks. I've never liked my playboy reputation and I particularly don't like it now that everything is in the past.'

'Why is it in the past?' she enquired.

'Because despite making it plain from the outset that I wasn't interested in true love—which I thought was honourable—there were often tears and recriminations, which made me feel like a heel. And because I became bored with the dating process. But also because having lived alone for so long I've grown to like my freedom. Now if I do have the occasional liaison it's with someone whom I *know* won't attempt to tie me down.'

She put the apple core aside. 'Did your wife marry again?'

'Yes, and because she was desperate to have more kids she got busy in that department straight away. Now she has another four, including the daughter whose rocking horse I was mending.'

'You're friendly with her and her husband?'

'I am. Polly's put on weight and I can hardly recognise her as the girl I once tried to tell myself I was in love with, but she's a cheery woman. She's never said anything bad about me to Russ. I'll always be grateful for that. Bedtime,' he decreed, when she yawned.

Jennet nodded. All of a sudden she felt sleepy.

'You're not going to spend the night on the sofa,' Connor said, when she started to plump up the cushions. 'You can use my bed and I'll come in here.'

'No, thanks.'

'Yes, and forget about being stubborn.'

Standing up, she shook out the blanket. 'Look, this is my house and—'

'You're arguing with an injured man?' He hoisted himself up onto his crutches.

'No, he's arguing with me. But it's too late to argue.'

'Much too late. Now's the time for obedience and brute strength,' he declared, and, hooking a muscled arm and a crutch around her, he started to hoick her towards the bedroom.

Half lifted off her feet, Jennet wriggled, but she could not escape. His hold was firm and as he hop-swung along he was trundling her with him.

'Connor, let me go!' she protested.

'The only way I'll do that is if you push me over,' he said, manoeuvring them in through the door. 'And you won't because you don't want me with two busted legs.'

'You think so?'

'I know so.' He had brought them beside the bed, where he stopped. 'Oh, sweetheart,' he said, looking down at her.

As she followed his gaze, her eyes widened. Somewhere amidst her wriggling and his manhandling, the strap of her nightdress had slipped again, the bodice had twisted and now one firm round breast was revealed. Amidst the manhandling she had also become aroused and her nipple was rigid.

'No,' he commanded, when she made to cover herself. His grey eyes burned into hers. 'I want to taste you,' he murmured, and he lowered his head and lapped the tip of his tongue across the wine-red point.

Jennet quivered. His moist touch seemed the height of eroticism. She felt her breasts swell in response and an ache tug between her thighs. She accepted the caress for a few delicious moments then, fisting her hands in the darkness of his hair, she directed his mouth to her other hungering breast.

'Please,' she said.

He licked at the cockled peak and a sensual tide swept through her. A thousand forgotten feelings came alive. She loosened her grip and as he straightened up her hands slid down to rest on his shoulders.

'I think we should sleep in my bed—together,' Connor said, 'and indulge in some "knotting and gendering," as I believe Shakespeare said.'

Her heart jackhammered. An inner voice warned that she did not want to start on an affair and would be playing with fire... but it echoed away into the silence. She could not fight her desire. Alone with him in the middle of the night in Capri, all resistance had gone.

'I think so too,' she told him, then suddenly frowned. 'What about your leg?'

'The muscle may be torn, but all the other parts of me are in working order,' he said, and, letting a crutch fall, he wound one arm around her and pulled her close.

Sliding his hand down her back, he grasped the round of her buttock and drew her into his loins. She gulped in air. Their clothes were thin and his arousal branded a fiery baton against her stomach.

'In—in magnificent working order,' she said jerkily.

Connor grinned. 'Flatterer,' he said.

The other crutch fell away and he placed his hands one on either side of her face, threading them into her thick brown hair. He looked gravely down, then his mouth sought hers. There was a desperate crushing of lips and tongues. A wild kissing. A moist devouring. Her hands tightened on his shoulders.

'Whoa,' he said finally, taking a ragged breath.

Easing back a fraction of an inch, he licked his tongue around the rim of her lips and she recognised that he was regulating and tenderly cooling their passion.

'Let's take this off,' he murmured, and she felt him easing the pink material up over her hips. 'I want to look at you.'

Together they drew the nightgown off over her head and as it fell in a shimmering heap his eyes moved slumberously over her. Jennet felt a heady delight at being the object of his scrutiny, the object of his desire. He lifted a hand and drew it slowly down, feather-stroking the tips of his fingers over the swollen spheres of her breasts, across the flatness of her stomach and to the triangle of dark curls which nestled between her thighs.

'You are exquisite,' Connor said, and smiled. 'But this standing up business is getting to me again, so let's lie down.'

Stretching out on the bed, she waited as he joined her more slowly.

'What are you doing?' he asked as she reached out an arm.

'Switching off the lamp.'

'You prefer to make love in the dark?'

'No, I don't, but—'

'Your husband did?'

'Well—yes.'

Lying on his side, he looked at her across the pillow. 'Touch brings pleasure,' he said, 'but vision can heighten the sensation.' He stroked his fingers along the silken underside of one breast and around to the puckered point. 'At least, it does for me.'

Jennet flattened a hand on his chest and lightly scoured it across first one flat brown nipple and then the other.

'And me,' she told him huskily.

They kissed again and his mouth began a slow, sweet journey. He kissed her throat, her breasts, her stomach and her thighs.

'Hey, what's this?' Connor said, all of a sudden. He placed a hand on her hip and rolled her forward. 'A tattoo?'

Her heart sank. Wound up in her desire, she had forgotten about the tiny butterfly. 'You don't care for it?' she asked, looking at him with wary green eyes.

'On the contrary, I think it's great. Though I'd have gone for two tap-dancing spaghetti hoops.'

Jennet started to laugh, a low, delighted gurgling laugh of relief. 'Maybe I will, next time.'

'You could have them here,' he said, taking a mock bite out of her posterior. 'Or here.' He nibbled at her waist. 'Or here.' He pressed his face into the scented valley between her breasts.

His movements were slowing, deepening, as desire returned. He began kissing and licking and mouthing her body again. She closed her eyes. He had lips which seemed to know exactly where to linger, fingers which knew exactly where to touch. She trembled. A pulse was throbbing deep inside her, and as his hand slid between her thighs, seeking the moist velvet of her femininity, she arched up against him.

'I've needed this for so long,' she said.

'And I've wanted you ever since you kissed me. Ever since we kissed,' he adjusted, when she prodded him with a protesting finger. 'Ever since I became aware of you as a gorgeous, delectable, living, breathing *woman.*'

'You thought I was a cardboard cut-out before?' Jennet teased.

'No, but—' Lifting his hips, he slid off his shorts.

'Shall I come on top of you?' she said. 'Would it be easier?'

'It would, but not yet.'

'No?'

Connor smiled. 'There's no rush. One of the advantages to reaching my great age is that you learn a degree of control—and we have the rest of the night.'

He took hold of her hand and guided it down between their bodies. When she wound her fingers around the thrust of his manhood and stroked him, he drew in a shuddering breath. Telling her to hold him tighter, he submitted to her pleasuring until he felt his need threaten to overwhelm him.

'Jennet,' he muttered, and held her fingers still.

His mouth went again to her breast. He suckled, drawing on first one sensitive point and then the other until she began to gasp, uttering little animal sounds and rolling her head from side to side on the pillow.

'Please,' she said, through clenched teeth.

He opened the drawer in the bedside table. 'Protection,' he explained, and when he was ready she straddled him.

He positioned her and as she felt him slide into her her hips began to rock. Her stomach muscles tightened and her heart threatened to explode within her chest. Her breath was coming far too quickly.

'Connor...I...' Her body jerked. Stars burst behind her closed eyelids. There was a rush, a flooding deep inside her. 'I'm sorry,' she said, wilting against him.

He curled a hand around her neck, drawing her closer.

'Don't be sorry. It'll happen again.'

'But—'

He captured the fullness of her lower lip between his teeth to stop her from talking and his hands moved over her again, exploring, seeking, caressing. Jennet had believed her desire must be sated, but soon he had aroused her again. And this time the arousal was deeper, stronger, more intense.

A knee on either side of him, she bent forward and he feasted on her breasts. As his mouth tugged at the rigid points, she clutched at his shoulders, her nails biting in.

'You were right—it *is* happening again,' she gasped.

'And it's happening for me,' Connor said, his voice a growl amidst the rough drag of his breathing.

Their hips moved in the rhythm of love. Faster and faster. The beat of their bodies matched, and, in a giddying moment of sensation when Jennet felt as if she was disintegrating into a million wondrous pieces, they became one.

CHAPTER SIX

SLIDING two hands beneath the heavy fall of spice-brown hair, Jennet lifted it free from the back of her neck. She closed her eyes and raised her face to the sun. She sighed. A light breeze brushed over her skin like warm silk. Heat seeped deep into her bones. The only sound was the idle suck and fall of waves on the shingle.

'Better than bashing away at the typewriter?' Connor said, beside her.

Her lips spread into a smile. 'Much.'

When they had awoken that morning, the rain had stopped and the sun was shining. And because they had slept longer than usual, the workmen had arrived. Anxious to ask them to take a look at the roof and full of sudden misgivings about having spent the night in Connor's bed, she had sped upstairs to her room and dressed. As the extent of repairs had been assessed, they had eaten breakfast and gone their separate ways. She had sat down at the kitchen table and reread the dialogue which she had written the previous day, while her guest—her *lover*—had gone to wield his paintbrush.

Around noon Connor had called down to ask if she could spare a minute sometime and, grateful for the diversion—any diversion—she had promptly joined him.

'All done,' he had announced, back-handing a smear of apricot-white from his chin.

She had admired the room, which now seemed twice as light and spacious, thanked him for his efforts and, when he had told her that she could return to work, had made a face.

'You've finished, it's a lovely day, so why don't we have lunch and go for a walk?' she had suggested. 'Not too far away, there's a tiny beach which Stuart and I discovered. You could probably manage to get down there.'

Taking it slowly and sometimes stopping to allow him to rest on his crutches, they had followed a path which wound down through ancient untended olive groves until they had reached a wooded cleft in the coast. Here a series of shallow earth steps led down to a secluded cove. And here they were, sitting on the shingle.

Jennet opened her eyes. 'There wasn't much type-writer-bashing being done,' she confessed. 'Maybe it was because the workmen were forever climbing up and down ladders and making a noise, but I couldn't seem to concentrate and never really got going.'

'Or perhaps it was because you had other things on your mind?' Connor suggested.

Her heart lurched. Dark glasses obscured the expression in his eyes, yet the husky timbre of his voice had made his meaning plain. And thoughts of their lovemaking had intruded all morning: the release she had felt after three long empty years, the ecstasy... and the doubts.

She attempted a careless shrug. 'Could be.'

'The inspiration'll flow tomorrow,' he said. 'And if it doesn't we can always take another walk or—' he slid her a grin '—I'll pluck up my courage, down a couple of stiff drinks and let you carry me off on the scooter for some sightseeing.'

'You're not cracking the whip?' she asked, tempted by his suggestion, and thinking that this was the first time since she had started writing *Hutton's Spa* that she had felt any inclination to take time off.

'No need. There're episodes stacked up and you work damned hard and if the eager beaver had a break it'd help recharge her batteries.'

What he said was true, yet the notion that he might not want her to persevere *too* determinedly with the Beth/ Dinsdale draft intruded. Jennet sat straighter. She would finish it as soon as possible.

'I'm going to work tomorrow,' she declared.

Pulling off his black knit sports shirt, he spread it out on the shingle behind him. 'Up to you,' he said easily, and lay down.

Ever since waking from what he had declared was his best night's sleep in weeks, Connor had been an amiable and light-hearted companion. And now, as he soaked up the sun, he was contented.

'Why were you so reluctant to come to Capri?' she enquired.

'Because of us.' He pulled his dark glasses down his nose and looked sombrely at her over the top. 'I had a suspicion we'd wind up in bed—which is why I took the precaution of buying protection—but I was worried about us becoming personally involved because we need to work together. Business with pleasure can be a difficult mix.'

Jennet frowned down at him. 'That's why you were tense?'

'Yes. But now...' He stretched lazily, the satisfied tiger. 'Now I realise that we're both sensible adults who can handle the situation.'

Drawing up her legs, she wrapped her arms around them and rested her chin on her knees. She was not sure she was sensible. Or had been. Connor's statement made it clear that he expected their physical involvement to continue. She gazed out across the shimmering sea. Did *she* want it to continue?

The obvious answer had to be no. She felt uncomfortable with the idea of having an affair, especially one which she knew in advance would lead nowhere. Her insides hollowed. It had also occurred to her that maybe—just maybe—he had made love with the idea of softening her up in case he returned to his request that she write an older woman/younger man romance. Was he instigating a sexual control?

So should she announce that last night, whilst wonderful, had been a one-night stand? Her first ever, Jennet thought wryly. Did she say that, sorry, she believed a sexual connection would be damaging and suggest that he arrange a flight home? She fingertipped a slick of perspiration from her brow. Ending their entanglement before it had a chance to develop and *hurt* seemed the sensible action, so why was she dithering? What was she hoping for?

'Are you going in for a dip?' Connor enquired.

'I'd like to,' she replied, eyeing the crystal-clear water which looked temptingly cool and inviting. 'But I didn't bring a costume.'

'You don't need one. We're here alone, so the only people who could see you *au naturel* would be a boatload of trippers *if* they happened along and *if* they came in close.' He wiggled his eyebrows. 'And, of course, me.'

'I'd make an old man very happy?'

'Less of the old. I'm in my prime,' he protested, in mock reprimand. 'But yes. Why don't you swim?' Sitting up, he indicated his shirt. 'You can dry yourself on that.'

She hesitated. She could remember other visits to the sheltered beach when her inclination had been to peel off her clothes and plunge into the water; but she never had. She climbed to her feet. She was damned if she would be the shrinking violet now.

'I will,' she decided.

In a spirit of defiance, Jennet stripped off her floral yellow pinafore dress, the little white top which she wore beneath it, her white lacy bra and briefs. She had, after all, been naked with him in bed. He had, after all, kissed virtually every inch of her skin, she rationalised.

'Happy?' she asked as she twisted her hair into a makeshift knot on the top of her head.

Connor grinned. 'Every man in the world appreciates a good naked female body and yours is—' he kissed his fingers '—*delizioso*. Ever thought of auditioning for *Baywatch*?'

She laughed and shook her head. 'Not top-heavy enough, though I could always arrange some surgical enhancement.'

'No way. Those two beautiful handfuls fit perfectly into my hands; they are just right.'

'Thank you, kind sir,' she said, smiling, and waded out into the sea.

'Don't go too far out,' he called, a few minutes later. 'I don't want to have to dive in, plaster and all, and rescue you.'

She swam closer to shore, feeling the cool swirl of the water all around her. 'I'm safe,' she said, 'and it's bliss.'

'I wish I could come in with you.'

'In your birthday suit?'

'For sure.'

Jennet grinned. 'So do I.'

His open appreciation of her figure and easy acceptance of the sexual force had created a go-anywhere, try-everything, all-is-possible kind of a mood. A buzz.

He made her feel good to be alive. She splashed with her feet. Good to be a young, shapely and desired woman.

She swam a little longer, then made for the beach. Her head held high, she strode out of the sea. The prospect of standing naked in front of him was making her heart flutter like a caged bird, yet she walked with pride.

'Sweet mercy,' Connor murmured. He watched the water trickling down her body, over the high globes of her breasts, across her stomach and into the dark furred triangle between her thighs. 'You're turning me on something rotten.'

Jennet chuckled. She liked his confidence to joke about his arousal and his lack of inhibition. She also liked the look of him—his lithe body, the hair on his chest which gleamed in the sunshine, his careless feline sprawl. A bead of sweat formed at his throat and she watched it trickle in a slow path down his chest.

'My heart bleeds,' she said pertly.

'So it should,' he responded, handing her his shirt. 'I'd put myself out of my agony and take you right now, only the pebbles are hard and that boatload of trippers might appear. And—the crunch—if I did I doubt I'd ever find the energy to haul myself back up to the villa.'

'Excuses, excuses,' she chanted, and started to dry herself.

'You didn't swim in the nude when you came here with your husband?' he enquired.

She stepped into her lacy briefs. 'No. I suggested it, but he wouldn't agree. Stuart was conservative and could be... strait-laced.'

'Which is why he preferred the light off when you made love?'

'Yes.' Leaning forward, she dipped her arms through the straps of her bra and fastened it behind her back. 'He also hated my tattoo, which I had done in a mad moment when I was on holiday once with a girlfriend. He thought it looked cheap and if we went swimming—'

'In swimsuits?' Connor put in drily.

'Always—he insisted on my covering it with sticking plaster. But, even though he could be strait-laced, he was good company and had a sense of humour.' Defiance lit a green fire in her eyes. 'We were happy.'

'But?'

Jennet hesitated, pulling on the white top and her pinafore. 'Our marriage wasn't as easy and sharing as I'd expected it to be,' she said, as though the words were being dragged out of her. 'I think the trouble was that I fell in love with the image I had of him as loyal and steady, rather than with Stuart himself. He was loyal and steady, but—' she gnawed at her lip '—I don't want to be *dis*loyal—but he had a tendency to take things so seriously.'

'For example?'

She made a face. 'He worried about his pension and was pernickety about his vitamin intake.'

'How old was he?'

'The same age as me—twenty-seven when we married.'

'How did you meet your husband?'

She loosened her topknot and started to blot at her hair with the shirt. She had kept her head out of the water, so only stray tendrils were damp.

'We met when he was selling my mother's house in Sussex before she moved to Portugal, where she lives now. Stuart was an estate agent, and the advice he gave and his handling of the transaction were level-headed and thorough. He seemed so stable and I was focused on stability.'

'A reaction against your mother's lightweight men,' Connor observed, picking up a handful of fine shingle and sifting it through his fingers.

Jennet frowned. 'Yes.'

'Didn't him being . . . prim and proper irritate you?'

She nodded ruefully. 'Though I never admitted how much until after he'd died. And I wasn't irritated at first. In fact, it amused me when he became prudish and would lay down the law. It was such a change to the free-wheeling existence which I'd been used to and it seemed to show that he cared.' She finger-combed through the tousled brown strands. 'Though it didn't amuse me so much when he objected to my writing.'

'That's why you stopped? And why did he object?'

'Stuart was suspicious of writing. He classified it as "arty crafty" and felt it wasn't an entirely kosher activity, plus he thought that I should spend the time when I wasn't at work looking after the house and looking after him.' She moved her shoulders. 'He had a point.'

'You didn't insist on continuing to write?'

'No. We were newly married when he vetoed it and I wasn't inclined to argue. I realise how weak that sounds now, but I wanted to please him. Ready to go?'

Connor reached for his crutches and hauled himself upright. 'I get the impression that you rarely argued with your husband,' he said as they started to make their way up through the trees.

'Almost never.'

'But there've been times when you've done nothing *but* argue with me,' he demurred.

'That's different.'

'How? Because we're not man and wife? So you'll obey without question if I slip a ring on your finger?'

Jennet's heart missed a beat. 'No chance.'

He slid her a dry look. 'I thought not.'

'When we argue, the anger is out in the open and afterwards it's over,' she said. 'But if I objected to something which Stuart said he didn't protest, flare up and come back with his opinion, he sulked. He'd sulk for days and sometimes didn't thaw out for weeks. Or ever. Like when I told him I wouldn't sell Tommaso's villa. He never properly forgave me for that.'

'But he must've enjoyed coming to Capri,' Connor protested. They had reached open land and he stopped, his eyes travelling across the lush green stretch of fields and down to the sparkling sapphire-blue sea. 'Even though he disagreed, he must've admitted that owning a house here did have its attractions.'

She gave a sad flash of a smile. 'No. Stuart didn't care for Italy. He thought the people were too easygoing and everything was too lax. It wasn't his kind of place. He saw no joy in my owning the villa, but then neither would he have seen any joy in owning the house which I have back home.'

His brow furrowed. 'Why ever not?'

'He'd have said that because it doesn't have double glazing and central heating it would be difficult to sell and so was a bad buy. But I'm glad I bought it,' she said, her voice suddenly fierce. 'I feel at home there, whereas I always had a sense of rattling around in the modern house.'

'The house which had been your husband's choice?'

'Yes.' She made a wry grimace. 'It met all his requirements.'

'You weren't prepared to put your foot down and object?' he said as they resumed their journey. 'Even if it did result in him going off in a sulk or maybe having a ding-dong row?'

'No, and we never had a ding-dong row. Correction, we didn't until the night that he was killed.' Anguish darkened her eyes. 'If we hadn't been quarrelling, Stuart would never've walked off into the road and he would've heard the car and—' Jennet broke off. As it always did, the memory of the fatal evening had balled into a suffocating mass inside her chest.

'Accidents happen,' Connor said gently.

'Yes, but if I hadn't lost my temper—if I'd kept calm, then—'

'You blame yourself and you're all torn up about it?' He stopped to put a hand on her arm. 'Jennet, you shouldn't be. You mustn't be. These things are—'

'I'd rather not talk about it,' she said, moving away and moving on. 'While you're here perhaps you'd like to visit the Villa of San Michele, which was the home of Axel Munthe?' she suggested. 'It's a lovely house, full of statues and with great views from the garden.'

He cast her a thoughtful look. 'I've read Munthe's book about his villa, so that'd be interesting,' he said.

Although Jennet had tried not to sound too critical, it had taken courage to admit that life with her husband had sometimes been difficult, Connor mused. Their marriage might have worked, yet it was obvious that she had *made* it work and he had no doubt that, if she had not been widowed, she would have doggedly continued to make it work.

She had survived the hurly-burly of her adolescence with remarkable equanimity, yet she was not unscathed.

Like everyone else, she carried emotional baggage. Hers included the determination that when she married it would be for keeps. After seeing her mother's marriages fail, albeit amicably, and the other toings and froings, it had become essential to her that she had a lasting relationship. Come what may.

He frowned. He understood her need, and yet, if her husband had not been killed, his narrow-minded and dogmatic ways would have destroyed her spirit. With his sulking—which must have been wearing to live with and made her think twice about upsetting him—he would have quelled her natural fire.

Stuart Galbraith had also been blind to her sensuality and her glorious abandon. The fool! he thought angrily. Jennet would have been trapped in a restrictive marriage which was destined to become lacklustre. He narrowed his eyes against the rake of the sun. Whilst the young man's death had been tragic, in his opinion she had had a lucky escape.

'No ill effects from the walking?' Jennet enquired.

They were sitting on the terrace, drinking after-dinner coffee and watching the sun turn a deep glowing orange as it sank slowly in the sky.

'None.' He flexed his shoulders, kneaded the back of his neck and continued, 'Though having to lift a hundred and ninety pounds each time I move is starting to beef up the muscles, so by the end of three weeks I could be splitting out of my shirts.'

'Like the Incredible Hulk,' she teased, eyeing the shoulders beneath his collarless white shirt. At the sound of hammering, she turned to look up at the roof. 'They seem determined to finish tonight.'

Having decided on the number of roof tiles which needed to be replaced, the workmen had proceeded to refloor her balcony. This had taken until late afternoon, when they had driven off in their van. New tiles were to be purchased from a nearby builder's yard, yet it had been two hours before they had returned, full of silver-tongued apologies for an unexplained delay.

'We fix roof now,' they had declared, and had been crawling around, prising off and replacing, ever since.

'Telephone,' Connor said abruptly, tilting his head.

Going through to the living room, Jennet lifted the receiver. 'It's your son,' she called, a moment or two later.

Grinning, he swung in through the French windows. 'At last.'

'I'm going to have a shower,' she said as he picked up the phone. 'I'll be down later.'

Jennet showered, shampooed her hair and towelled herself dry. She stroked her fingers along her bare arms. Before she had been sticky with salt, but now her skin felt smooth. She stepped into fresh briefs—the leopardskin-print ones—picked up a comb and walked to the sliding glass doors which stood open onto the balcony. She smiled. The new floor of deep red glazed tiles was far smarter than the weather-faded mottled green.

She listened, heard nothing and peeped out. A lack of ladders said that the workmen had gone and the silence meant Connor had ended his call. Going to the waist-high wall, she peered down at the terrace. She could not see him, but perhaps he had gone into the kitchen to get himself a drink. After coffee, he sometimes had a brandy.

She gazed out at the sunset. The orange ball of the sun hovered on the horizon and the sky was a sheet of gold. Lemon-gold up high and progressing down through translucent shades of primrose, jasmine and saffron, until it met the sea in a mustard line. The gold coloured the world, gilding the garden below, the rolling fields, the face of a distant cliff.

Jennet began to comb through her hair. Today was the first time she had talked about Stuart and their marriage, she thought as she eased away tangles. She had not meant to be as forthright—nor so brutally honest— but sharing her thoughts had helped her to put the past into perspective. Her combing slowed. Though she had not told Connor everything.

Connor. Her thought train jumped tracks. His comment about putting a ring on her finger had caused a flurry of emotion inside her. Why? The remark had been casual and, besides, rings on fingers meant love and love did not feature in their equation. The personal side of their relationship was based on lust.

And the working side? What would she do if he rejected the draft she was writing and insisted on a toyboy affair? Her hair was combed back from her brow. She had insisted she would pull out, but, as well as relinquishing vital future pay cheques, withdrawing could mean the end of her writing career. Word of her strong-headedness and unreliability would be bound to spread to other TV companies who would then be unwilling to employ her.

As a pad-pad of crutches sounded, Jennet stood bolt upright.

'Don't you know how to knock?' she demanded, turning her head to glare at the man who had arrived behind her. The man who possessed the power to wreck her livelihood. 'First you make a fist and rap your knuckles on the door, then you wait to be invited in.'

'You're too keyed up,' Connor protested.

'I'm not keyed up!'

'I did knock, but you were obviously so busy thinking that you didn't hear me.'

'Oh. Sorry,' she mumbled. She put the comb on the balcony wall. Her hair was halfway to being dry now. 'Why are you here?' she asked, looking out at the sky.

If she faced him, naked apart from the high cut briefs, there would be a sexual reaction between them. It was a reaction which she preferred to avoid.

'I came to tell you the workmen have finished, in total.' Stretching past her, he laid his sticks against the wall then slid one arm around her waist and looped the other in front of her, across her shoulders. He was keeping his balance—and holding her. 'I also came to say that I passed on your invitation to Russ and he'll be arriving the day after tomorrow, to stay for three days. I trust that's OK?'

'It is.' Jennet stood stiffly. 'How is he?'

'Still not been held at gunpoint and still having a whale of a time. He's in Northern Italy now, minus the Danish boys who've gone elsewhere, but meeting other backpackers along the way.'

'I'll make up a bed in the spare room,' she declared.

'Tomorrow,' Connor said.

She looked straight ahead. An arrow of birds was winging its way homewards across the golden, but darkening sky.

'And rehang the curtains,' she continued.

His hand slid from her waist and started to move slowly, slowly, down over her hip bone and towards her thigh. Outwardly she remained impassive, yet her heart was banging like a drum. Conflicting voices jarred in her head—one ordering her to break away, the other insisting that she needed his touch.

She drew in a breath. 'And I must—'

His hand stilled. 'You are keyed up,' he said. 'It comes and goes, but you're keyed up about us. I understand that you're hooked into your career and don't want too many distractions, so—' he paused '—why don't we treat this as a holiday romance and when we get back home—?'

'It's forgotten and we revert to our usual working relationship,' Jennet completed, clutching thankfully at the idea.

She had had to make a decision and he was offering her one. Indeed, his reference to a holiday romance indicated that he, too, must be having second thoughts about an ongoing entanglement.

There was a moment of silence behind her. 'Sure,' Connor agreed, his tone level and conveying no emotion. His hand began to slide downwards again. 'I also came because I want to make love to you.'

'Here?' she asked, her voice suddenly throaty. 'Now?'

'Here and now,' he confirmed. 'A sad addiction which has assaulted me ever since we were at the beach, but, alas, I was forced to wait until we were alone.'

As he drew aside her hair to press his lips to the side of her neck, her pulses quickened. This might be a short-lived affair, yet she wanted him with a desire, a *passion* which was already trembling through her body.

'I like the smell of your hair. I like the fragrance of your skin, the fragrance and taste of you,' he said softly, and his other hand moved to her breast, to cup the burgeoning globe, to mould and caress.

Her heart broke into an erratic beat. Stuart had never aroused her so quickly, she thought, but then he had never lifted her to such passionate heights as Connor had done last night. Her eyes drifted closed. Now her only awareness was of him. The warmth of his mouth on her neck, the touch of his hands, the latent energy of the male body which was pressed against hers.

As his finger probed beneath the edge of her panties, Jennet gasped. She arched her spine. His thumb was grazing across the tiny pink beak of her sex and her desire grabbed, sharpened, *howled*. Flattening the hand at her breast, he scoured it across the straining peak and as she felt the smooth, hard circling of his palm she gasped again.

'Off,' he murmured, easing down her panties.

Eyes still closed, she wriggled and stepped out. His touch was freer now and more erotic. Her nerve impulses seemed electrical. He was bringing her deftly and torturously to the brink—that delicious brink.

As his fingers moved—delicately, but relentlessly—in a mesmeric motion at her breast and in the moistened valley of her groin, she drew in a breath. Seeking a measure of control, she lifted her lids and saw that the golden sky had deepened into mauve. A haze covered the land in grey chiffon. It was twilight.

The tempo of his caressing fingers increased, his touch imperceptibly strengthened. He was driving her on and on. Now her entire body was tingling. Adrenalin sped through her veins. Her skin throbbed with heat. Jennet trembled. She had reached the brink and, as his long finger explored the silken secrecy of her thighs and his palm circled on her swollen nipple, she gasped and tumbled over.

He held her quietly for a second or two, then drew back. There was the rasp of the zip of his jeans, a preparation, then he was parting her legs and slipping inside her. She clenched her teeth. He felt so hard, so hot, so filling.

He shifted to please them both and bent, his long body against her spine.

Jennet spread her hands on the top of the wall. He was moving—sliding and thrusting with increasing need, sending currents of sensation shuddering through her. He rounded both hands on her breasts, rolling and pinching at her nipples with the same quickening force.

She whimpered. She was teetering on the edge, dangling over the precipice, caught on that bitter-sweet see-saw.

'Jennet,' he said, in a low, guttural voice.

For a tense, controlling moment, he held himself still. Then his body bucked against hers, the see-saw tipped and she was flying out into the violet dusk. Spinning and twirling. Reaching, reaching, reaching...and finding.

Jennet had dressed after their lovemaking and was going to join him on the terrace when the telephone rang again.

'Mitch has gone,' her mother announced as she lifted the receiver. 'We had a humdinger of a quarrel and he threw all his belongings into his car and drove off.'

She raised weary eyes to the ceiling. The romantic tussles had been too repetitive over the years to be of any great concern any longer—and especially not right now.

'He'll be back,' she said.

Other men had made similar gestures, yet they had inevitably appeared on the doorstep not much later. And inevitably it had been Tina who, in her own sweet time and with sweet regrets, had sent them on their way.

'I shan't take him back. I want to be alone for a while and have some peace and quiet.'

'Since when?' Jennet enquired wryly.

As soon as one amour ended, her mother moved on to the next and had never been on her own for more than a few weeks. As for peace and quiet—if she stayed in for three consecutive evenings she became restless.

'Since I decided to write my autobiography,' came the declaration.

She gave a hoot of incredulous laughter. 'You—write a book? Be serious. You've never written anything longer than a letter in your life.'

'Even so, I think I could do it. The media are still interested in me and it'd be fun to take a trip down memory lane.' Her mother chuckled. 'Fun to tell all my stories.'

'Fun for you perhaps,' she said, rapidly sobering, 'but not for others. You might reveal episodes which people would rather forget, which could embarrass them or cause distress to their partners.'

'I'll skip anything sensitive,' came the casual reply.

'Writing your autobiography would be a major operation. It'd take ages and be hard work.'

'Ages?'

'I reckon it'd take you at least a year,' Jennet said, and heard an intake of breath. 'You realise you'd need to be accurate on dates and facts?' she ploughed on earnestly. 'And would have to make sure you didn't libel anyone, because otherwise you could wind up being sued? Think again. And think again about Mitch.'

'Maybe I shall,' her mother said slowly, 'about Mitch. But I intend to try with a book and if I get fed up—well, there's nothing lost. I've been looking through my diaries and photograph albums and I'll start making notes tomorrow.'

'But—'

'I'll keep you posted, Jay. Bye.'

Jennet replaced the receiver. 'Damn,' she muttered. 'Damn, damn, damn.'

'I helped myself,' Connor said, when she went out onto the terrace. He showed her the brandy goblet which he was nursing. 'Are you going to have a drink?'

'Later,' she said distractedly.

'Is something the matter?' he asked. 'I couldn't help hearing that you sounded agitated.'

'It's my mother. She's threatening to write her autobiography and I was trying to stop her.'

'You reckon she'd be wasting her time because no one would publish it?'

'No, I think it would be published.' She sat down on a chair beside him. 'You see, my mother is Tina Lemoine.'

He raised his brows, but said nothing.

'You know who I mean?' Jennet enquired.

'I do. I've seen her photograph in the paper and read about her being an icon of the sixties. You expect me to fall flat on my back and kick my legs up in the air?'

'No, but— You're not intrigued or impressed . . . or shocked? Most people are. Most people start asking me endless questions about her or spend for ever inspecting me to see whether or not I look like her.'

'Working in television, I've met my share of famous people—properly famous people,' he said, 'and I ceased to be impressed long ago.' He sipped at his brandy. 'You've kept quiet about your mother because you dislike being bombarded with questions?'

Jennet nodded. 'I didn't mind so much when I was a child, but as I grew older having to go through the same routine time and time again got me down. Though it's not just the questions I dislike, it's the way that once I reveal the relationship everyone seems to view me as Tina Lemoine's daughter and no longer as *me*.'

'And you'd prefer her not to publish her memoirs because that'd make it harder for you to remain anonymous?'

'Yes, and because—' A worried frown formed between her brows. 'Yes,' she said. 'You remember how I panicked when the guy from *The Comet* tried to take my photograph?'

Connor looked down at his leg, which rested on the footstool. 'As if I could forget,' he remarked drily.

'I panicked because the gossip columnist at the paper had been running a campaign to locate me,' she said, and explained. 'I thought I was safe and, as it turned out, I was, but if Tina should—'

'You call her Tina?' he cut in.

She nodded. 'She prefers it. If Tina writes her life story,' she continued, 'my identity will become common knowledge.'

'Hardly,' he protested. 'With all due respect, the book's not going to be a best-seller, so—'

'I have to make her change her mind,' Jennet insisted.

He sighed. 'You're overreacting.'

'Maybe. I will have a drink,' she said, and went through to the kitchen.

'Are we sleeping in my bed tonight or yours?' Connor enquired, a couple of hours later.

Her heart missed a beat. He lusted after her, but might he also be sleeping with her to make her more biddable in the future? Whatever the reason, she needed him.

'If we sleep in your bed it means you don't have to hop up the stairs,' she said.

'Mine it is.'

'And we'll keep to our own rooms while Russ is here.'

He shook his head. 'No.'

'No?' she protested.

'He's grown up now. He must know his father has needs, and if he doesn't it's high time he did.'

'But he's only staying for three nights.'

'And all we have together are two more weeks, so I'm going to sleep with you *every* night,' Connor rasped, his voice suddenly harsh. 'Understand?'

Jennet nodded. 'I understand,' she said.

CHAPTER SEVEN

CERISE, white, garnet, pale pink, magenta—the geraniums made a wall of vivid colour. Jennet stood patiently waiting as yet another tourist took yet another photograph of the terracotta troughs of flowers which filled the corner steps of the piazza and, when the shutter had clicked, walked on. As she approached the spread of sun-shaded, white-clothed tables, she smiled. When she had left her companion half an hour ago he had been eating ice cream, and he was still eating it.

'Decided to try the tutti-frutti,' Russ explained as she sat down beside him. He devoured another glacé-cherried and sultanaed spoonful. 'This Italian stuff is wicked. The cassata should be tasty too.'

'You're not planning on having a third bowl?' she protested.

He grinned. 'Then throw up over your shoulder when we're driving back on the scooter? Better not.'

'You're so thoughtful,' she said drily. Taking a box from the plastic bag which she carried, she opened it to show him a small metal sculpture. 'It's a good likeness?'

'It's brilliant,' he declared, picking up the figure and laughing. 'Dad'll love it.'

'I've booked a table for tomorrow evening, eight-thirty at a local bistro, and it's my treat. Thanks for telling me it's your father's birthday tomorrow,' she went on. 'He hadn't said a word.'

'Who wants to admit they've reached the big Four-O?' The youth slumped in his seat in a gesture of extravagant anguish. 'No one.'

'Forty isn't ancient and he's not exactly a geriatric,' she protested.

Russ looked at her and grinned. 'If you say so.'

Jennet thought of how Connor had made love to her three times the previous night—and suspected that his son could be obliquely referring to their intimacy too. They might not spend the day locked in a clinch, but the sexual attraction which zinged between them must be discernible in the looks which they exchanged, in the smiles and occasional touches. Besides which he knew they shared a bed.

As her companion finished off his ice cream, she studied him. With short dark razored hair which hung over his brow, spaniel-brown eyes and a ready smile, he must turn female teenage legs to jelly. His good looks came straight from his father, yet his features were gentler. His personality was gentler too, she mused. He appeared to have missed out on Connor's driving ambition and steely streak.

'I'm glad Dad decided to let us meet,' Russ remarked as they set off back towards the passageway where she had parked the scooter. 'He's always kept his girlfriends hidden before.'

Unsure about being classified as a girlfriend and yet feeling unable to protest, she nodded. 'I've enjoyed meeting you too.'

'Put it there,' he instructed, stopping to press the flat of his hand against hers in grinning friendship. 'It's odd,' he continued as they walked on. 'Dad's such a cool dude. I mean, like, he hangs loose and I always have a monster time when I'm with him. It's a relief to get away from

Mum and her "wipe your feet" moaning,' he told her confidentially. 'Yet he's real particular about some things, like not living with anyone, and—' Russ groaned '—he has this massive guilt-trip about being divorced.'

Jennet swung him a look. She sensed an opportunity to—OK, meddle in matters which were none of her business, but maybe also to help.

'Whilst he regrets failing at marriage, I don't think it's the divorce which your father feels guilty about,' she said, 'so much as how he left you when you were a little boy.'

His brows curled in puzzlement. 'You reckon? But it never bothered me.'

'It didn't? How was that?' she prompted.

'Well, the way I saw it—'

As they drove back to the villa, the youth talked on and she listened.

Connor took a deep breath and blew. The flames of the four candles bent, flickered—and went out.

''Appy Birthday, *signore*,' said the elderly waiter who had carried in the blue and white iced cake with much ceremony.

'Happy Birthday,' chorused everyone in the small stone-walled bistro and applauded.

Smiling, he acknowledged the general good wishes and gave his thanks.

'Pity they couldn't fit on the correct number of candles,' Russ remarked as the diners returned to their meals, 'but the cake would've had to have been enormous.'

'Watch the lip,' Connor warned, in mock anger.

'"Time's winged chariot", alas,' Jennet said, sighing noisily. 'How does it feel to be middle-aged?'

His grey eyes met hers in a heavy-lidded look which made her heart race. 'I'll tell you later,' he said, and, sliding his hand around the back of her neck to draw her closer, he kissed her on the lips.

The waiter looked wistfully on. He could remember being young and in love—just. 'I go cut,' he announced as they broke apart, and carried the cake away.

'Thanks again for my presents,' Connor said. 'Everything was terrific—the books, the booze, the Flintstones boxer shorts—' his smile swung between Jennet and his son '—but these have to be the best.'

She and Russ had decided to save a couple of gifts for the evening celebrations and two metal sculptures sat on the table. One was a chubby Italian ice-cream vendor, complete with apron and boater, standing beside his cart. The other, which the craftsman had made to her specifications yesterday, was a man on crutches with his left leg in plaster.

'Too late now, but I should've suggested you got the guy to put a tortoise on his head,' Russ said, lifting up the miniature invalid.

'A tortoise?' she asked, puzzled.

'When I was a kid Dad used to put on a rubber shower cap in the shape of a tortoise and chase me around in it. I squealed blue murder. It was an ace game.'

Connor placed a despairing hand to his brow. 'That's my street cred ruined for all time,' he said.

She laughed. ''Fraid so.'

'You look credible right now,' Russ told him.

You look drop-dead *gorgeous*, Jennet thought. Earlier that evening, when she had come downstairs and found the guest of honour ready and waiting, she had done a double take. Connor had stood tall and broad-shouldered in an immaculate dark grey suit, a white shirt and a blue and yellow silk tie. She liked his casual elegance, but to see him so debonair and urbane—even on crutches—had made her heart pump furiously.

'You're not feeling traumatised from wearing a jacket and tie?' she enquired mischievously.

Grinning, he shot a snowy white cuff. 'A little.'

Russ turned to her. 'You look lovely,' he said.

She smiled. 'Thanks.'

She was wearing a short white sleeveless dress and strappy white high-heeled sandals. The dress, which tied on the shoulders, cinched her waist and skimmed her hips, accentuated the pale gold tan which she was acquiring. Being a brunette, she tanned easily. Her hair fell in an abundance of glossy brown curls around her shoulders and she had painstakingly made up her face: topaz eyeshadow, thick mascara, a touch of blusher high on her cheekbones and an amber lip-gloss. Gold earrings gleamed in her ears and there were golden chains at her throat and around her wrist.

'Dad has great taste,' the youth continued admiringly.

Connor covered her hand with his in a proprietorial gesture. 'And this is Dad's girl,' he said.

Russ grinned. 'You have a thing about older men?' he asked her.

'They do have certain…strengths,' she replied, her eyes sparkling.

'But we won't go into what those are right now,' Connor said, and indicated her empty glass. 'More wine?'

'Please. Yesterday Russ was saying how, when you went off to the States, he didn't feel he'd been abandoned or deprived,' she told him as he filled the glasses.

He frowned at his son. 'No?'

'Nope. I was only three and Mum was reassuring about how you still loved me, so I just accepted it. I suppose I must've missed you a bit, though I don't remember it—'

'Gee, thanks,' he muttered.

'—but by the time I reached five and went to school and had more need of a dad—for bonding and boasting about 'n stuff—you were back. Then, not much later, I had two dads.' The youth grinned. 'I couldn't lose. I reckon it was a good thing you left when you did,' he went on.

'How do you work that out?' Connor demanded.

'If you'd stayed at home any longer, you and Mum would've had rows. Right?'

He nodded. 'Big rows.'

'But you didn't. Some of my friends have had parents who shouted at each other and were hostile, and whether they were little kids at the time or teenagers it always upset them. I was never upset, because I never saw any fighting nor was aware of any bitterness. You may have screwed up by having to get married—which meant the odds were stacked against you—but you didn't screw *me* up,' Russ declared, and grinned. 'Here's the cake.'

The waiter served each of them with a slice of the rich fruit cake, then poured liqueurs which, he explained, came with the compliments of the house. As he departed, two girls who were seated at a nearby table raised their glasses.

'Congratulations,' they said.

Connor smiled and raised his glass in acknowledgement.

'You speak English?' Russ enquired, adjusting the collar of the red and blue striped rugby shirt which he wore with his best jeans.

He had noticed the girls when they had walked in. One was a plumpish brunette, while the other was a slender creature with long straight fair hair which fell halfway down her back. He had been sneaking glances at her, on and off, all evening and had noticed her glancing back at him.

The blonde smiled. 'We should. We're from New Zealand.'

'You're here on holiday?' he asked.

She nodded. 'Backpacking.'

'Me too,' he announced, as though the coincidence made them best mates. 'I've just crossed the South of France, calling in at—'

'Perhaps you'd like to take them some cake?' Jennet suggested, with a look at Connor who nodded.

Russ grinned. 'Please.' He carried over two plates, spoke to the girls and, a moment later, returned to collect his own. 'Going to discuss routes,' he explained, and went to join them.

'After all the years of beating myself up about leaving Russ, it turns out the impact was negligible and I was beating myself up over nothing,' Connor said, and managed a faintly ironic smile. 'I'd never have found the courage to raise the subject myself, so thank you for getting him to tell me.'

'Regard it as another present,' she said.

'It's a much valued one because it means that now I can stop carrying around all that guilt. I have a present for you,' he continued. 'This evening during the two hours it took you to get ready, I—'

'It took me less than one!'

'I read through what you've done on your Beth/ Dinsdale draft and—'

'You sneak!'

'Are you going to let me finish?' he enquired.

'Go ahead.'

'And I reckon their romance works. Superbly.'

'You do?' Jennet laughed with delight—and a great dollop of relief. 'So you'll scrap the toyboy idea?'

'For ever,' Connor said.

'I like you, I like you,' she burbled, and, stretching forward, she kissed him.

His lips were warm and tasted of liqueur. Seduced, she lingered, and the kiss lengthened. The press of mouth on mouth was beginning to inspire a sweet ache of longing when someone coughed close by.

'Excuse me.'

Jennet drew back, to discover that Russ was standing beside their table. She flushed. He had obviously spoken and was waiting for a reply.

'Sorry?' she said.

'When we were out yesterday we passed a disco which is around the corner from here. It has an arched entrance in a rough white wall, with a purple neon sign above it. What's it called?'

'La Dolce Vita,' she told him.

'The girls and I were thinking that we could all move on there.'

'Not me,' Connor said.

'You're too old for dancing?' Russ shrugged. 'Yup, I guess forty is—'

'I have a leg in plaster!' he protested.

'And I'm not keen to boogie on down, either,' Jennet told him.

'Why don't you go along with them?' Connor said, glancing towards the two girls who were expectantly watching on. 'You can make your own way back.'

'Thanks, I will. Could you leave a key under the mat?'

'No need,' Jennet said, opening her bag. 'I have a spare one. Enjoy.'

The youth slid her a wink. 'And you,' he said, and collected his partners and departed.

'Why didn't you tell me you'd be having a birthday?' she asked as they ate their cake.

'I was going to this morning and I intended to suggest we all go out for dinner,' Connor said, 'but you and Russ beat me to it.'

'So you don't mind being forty?'

He shook his head. 'I hated being thirty. It made me realise I'd stopped growing up and started growing old, but—'

'You suffered the black gloomies?' Jennet cut in. 'So did I.'

'But forty finds me in a state of the utmost well-being.' He ran a fingertip along the back of her hand. 'I wonder why?' he said, smiling into her eyes.

She knew it must be the general good mood of the evening which was affecting her—or perhaps the wine— but Connor seemed so affectionate, so fond, so...loving?

As they finished the cake, the waiter appeared with a tray of coffee and a dish of after-dinner mints.

'The guilt which I carried around over Russ was unnecessary,' Connor said, when they were alone again. 'And so is the guilt which you carry around about your husband's death. I know you find it a difficult subject, but won't you tell me what happened? Please?'

Jennet tensed. She preferred not to think about the long-ago evening, let alone talk about it, and yet the upward slant of his brows was beguiling. Should she take him into her confidence, again? For a moment, she dithered, then her shoulders were straightened. She would tell him what happened—though with certain limitations.

'We'd been out to dinner with a couple whom Stuart had met when he'd sold them a house—a huge place with stables and a swimming pool,' she began slowly. 'They were older than us—around fifty—and when they'd issued the invitation Stuart had said we ought to go because they'd shown some interest in buying a dress shop in the village for one of their daughters, which would mean business for him.'

'You didn't know them well?'

'I'd never met them before and I didn't like them. The man had made a fortune from selling kit cars, but he was a flash character and he and his wife didn't miss any opportunity to tell us how wealthy they were. They priced the designer clothes which they were wearing, showed us their five-thousand-pound watches, then moved on to holidays which they'd had in Bermuda and the Caribbean. They also boasted about a luxury yacht which they kept on the Costa del Sol.'

She stopped, frowned, and flattened out a square of silver foil from a mint which she had eaten. 'As we left their house we started to quarrel.'

'The ding-dong row?'

Jennet attempted a smile, but failed miserably. 'Yes. There were raised voices and high emotions which ended with Stuart stalking off along the middle of the road. The couple's drive had been filled with their collection of cars, so we'd left ours in a nearby lay-by. He was walking in the wrong direction, but I let him go. I started to look in my bag for my car keys, because I wasn't happy about him driving us home—'

'Had he been drinking?' Connor enquired.

'Yes. He wasn't drunk, but he'd had more than usual and I felt sure he'd be over the legal limit. I was looking in my bag,' she continued, 'when a white Mercedes shot past me in the dark and—' she winced '—a few seconds later I heard an almighty bump.'

'Your husband had been hit?'

She nodded. 'Apparently the car'd caught him a sideways blow which'd sent him flying. He'd been so wound up, he couldn't have heard it until it was too late. The Mercedes kept on going—'

'It was a hit-and-run?'

'Yes. The car was never traced and the police reckoned it'd probably been stolen. I saw Stuart lying on the road and was running towards him when a man who'd been out late-night jogging dashed up. He said he hadn't heard the Mercedes, either, but he'd seen the accident and he must've heard us rowing. He was very kind. He tried his best to resuscitate Stuart, but—' her throat had constricted and she needed to take a breath '—it was no use. He'd been killed outright.'

Connor squeezed her hand in sympathy and allowed her time to recover.

'What had you been quarrelling about?' he asked. 'Your hosts?'

'Them . . . and my mother.'

'Stuart didn't approve of her?'

Jennet screwed up the foil square into a tight ball. 'He used to criticise her for being far too fickle, too racy, but secretly the idea of having a celebrity mother-in-law gave him a buzz and whenever they met he was starry-eyed.'

'So what was the trouble? I wish you'd level with me,' he said, when she sat silent and taut and frowning.

She rolled the foil ball between her fingers. 'I can't. It's getting late. Shall we go?'

He nodded and drained his coffee cup.

'Please could I have the bill?' she asked the waiter, who was passing their table. 'And would you order us a taxi?'

The man smiled at her, but he spoke to Connor. '*Sì, signore,*' he said.

They were approaching the villa when another taxi passed them, coming back down the lane in the opposite direction.

'Russ must've returned,' Connor said, in surprise. 'And he and the girls seemed to be getting along so well.' As the driver slowed to a halt, he slid a hand inside his jacket. 'This is mine,' he told her, taking out his wallet. 'You paid for the meal, so don't argue.'

'No, sir, and thank you,' Jennet said, with a grin.

She had been worried that he might pursue his request for further details about the quarrel with Stuart, but, thankfully, he had let the matter lie.

Leaving her escort to settle the fare, she climbed out of the cab. She had reached the front door when a figure emerged from the shadows around the side of the house. It was a woman with a cloud of silvery blonde hair. She wore a grey silk trouser suit which showed off her slender frame to perfection and walked on perilously high heels.

Jennet stared. Talk of the devil, she thought. 'Tina!' she said.

'When you failed to answer both the bell and my shouts, I thought I'd need to spend the night on the doorstep,' the new arrival declared, in a voice which had been variously likened to a baritone sax and melted chocolate, but which was the result of smoking far too many cigarettes. She gave her a huge hug and kissed her. 'Mitch has gone, so I decided to come and seek comfort from my darling daughter. The journey was tedious, but never mind, I'm—'

A door slammed, the taxi moved away and Connor swung towards them through the darkness on his crutches.

'You're not alone,' her mother said, looking him interestedly up and down and smiling.

'This is Connor Malone. He's hurt his leg and is here for some rest and recuperation. Connor, this is my mother,' she said stiffly.

'Tall, dark and handsome,' Tina murmured, clasping the hand he had offered in both of hers. She smiled at Jennet. 'I should've guessed.'

'You've just arrived—from where?' he asked.

'Portugal. I must learn to travel lighter,' the visitor declared, and bent to lift a suitcase which sat to one side of the tiled frontage.

'Allow me,' he said as she sighed and wobbled on her high heels.

'When you're on crutches?'

'I can manage,' Connor assured her, and, shifting his sticks to one hand, he picked up the suitcase and hopped indoors.

'Three cheers for Sir Galahad,' Tina proclaimed, laughing as they followed him.

Jennet gave a razor of a smile. Her mother had a special quality of fragility to which men responded. She had seen her exploit it many times before and been wryly amused, but tonight the 'me, helpless woman, you, big strong male' routine infuriated her.

'Would you like something to eat or drink?' she enquired as she moved around the living room, switching
on lamps.

'Nothing, thanks. I ate on the plane and drank endless
cups of that vile coffee. But I'm dying for a cigarette.'
Dipping a hand into the grey suede pouch which she
carried, the new arrival produced a packet. 'I shall go
onto the terrace and light up.' She shone a smile of sweet
helplessness. 'Could someone open the doors?'

'I will,' Connor said, and duly obliged.

'You don't smoke?' Tina enquired, and he shook his
head.

'Neither should I.' She gave a deep, gushing laugh.
'But we all need some vices.'

'My vice right now would be a brandy. Please?' he
requested, speaking to Jennet.

'Coming up,' she replied, and walked away into the
kitchen.

Locating the bottle, she slammed it down on the table
and furiously twisted off the cap. She did not want her
mother here. Not now. She did not want her expecting
to be looked after, disrupting her work... and intruding
between her and Connor.

'Why didn't you tell your mother that I was here with
you?' he asked, trapezing in a minute or two later.

Jennet took a glass goblet from the cupboard. 'Because for the past three years she's been urging me to
find myself a man and if she'd known you were coming
to Capri she'd have decided we were lovers and nothing
I could say would've made her change her mind.'

He frowned. 'Would you like me to move in with Russ,
like us to sleep in separate rooms while she's here?'
hc suggested.

'No. We *are* lovers and I'm going to sleep with you every night,' she declared, her green eyes glittering. 'Understand?'

Connor looked at her, his eyes shrewd beneath straight black brows. 'I understand,' he said, and they went out onto the terrace.

'According to my calculations, you have two more weeks in Capri,' Tina declared, and nodded. 'That suits me.'

Jennet's teeth ground together. For her mother to have arrived without giving any warning had been bad enough, but the prospect of her being around for the entire remainder of *their* stay was worse. Much worse.

'I have a script to write,' she said, 'so I won't be available to make coffee and chat, and to go here, there and everywhere with you.'

Tina exhaled a plume of smoke. 'Connor could keep me company,' she said.

She felt a quick flare of absolute rage. She wanted to slap her mother, hard, for making the suggestion. She also wanted to slap Connor—for the inevitable agreement which she knew was coming.

'Sorry, I can't,' he said, and she looked at him in astonishment. 'I'm in the middle of painting the cellar and after that I'll be working on the bedroom where the rain leaked in. Trying to repay Jennet's hospitality,' he explained.

The new arrival pouted. 'Then I shall have a couple of days here and buzz off down the coast to stay with Silvio and his wife. Silvio is the brother of Tommaso, a delightful ex-husband of mine,' she told him.

'But it's ages since you've seen them,' Jennet said, frowning.

'Silvio and I get along wonderfully well together, Jay. You know we do. He'll be thrilled to see me.'

'Maybe, but—'

'I'm going. I've decided. There's no need for me to rush back to Portugal, not now that Mitch has gone for good.'

'For good?' she enquired.

'It should've been me who said it was over, but I met him down by the harbour a couple of days ago and he told me that he'd moved into his own apartment. So it's finished. Kaput. Mitch was my lover,' Tina told Connor conversationally. 'We'd been together for six months, but although he was a nice guy we didn't have that much in common.'

'Apart from in bed?' he said.

'It was all systems go there,' Tina declared, giggling like a naughty schoolgirl and slapping his thigh in mock reprimand for having brought up the subject. 'Mitch is younger than me and *so* energetic.'

'Younger?' he asked, shooting a quick look at Jennet.

'Fifteen, twenty years,' her mother declared, with a vague waft of the hand. 'It was Mitch's long blond hair which first attracted me. He's the twin of a fashion photographer whom I used to know. That guy wore a mink-lined bomber jacket, raced greyhounds and, like me, was game for anything. He raised hell every night.'

Connor lifted his brows. 'Sounds quite a character.'

'He was,' Tina said, and embarked on an amusing and risqué anecdote which had him laughing out loud.

When her story came to an end, she yawned. 'I need my beauty sleep, so if you'd care to tell me which room I'm in, Jay, I'll be off.'

'You're in my room,' Jennet said, rising. 'I'll make up the bed. Russ, Connor's teenage son, is in the spare room—and,' she added, a touch belligerently, 'we're sleeping downstairs.'

Her mother smiled. 'I see.'

'My son is out at a disco,' Connor said, 'so—'

'My kind of person,' Tina laughingly inserted.

'So if you hear footsteps in the middle of the night it'll be him arriving back.'

'Thanks for the warning, but—' a second yawn was patted away '—I'm sure I shan't hear a thing.'

'Why are you against your mother visiting Silvio?' Connor enquired, when Jennet climbed into bed beside him a short time later.

'Because she'll smile her flirty-flirty smile and Silvio'll start to pay court, and his wife will be hurt. It happens every time. And his wife is a kind, gentle woman who shouldn't have to go through that kind of emotional wringer.'

'Doesn't your mother care about how she feels?'

'She isn't even aware of it.'

'No? Can't you tell her?'

'I've tried umpteen times, but it's like riding an exercise bicycle to nowhere. Whatever I say, she laughs and dismisses her behaviour as harmless fun. And even if it dawned that it upsets Silvio's wife I doubt she'd consider it such a big deal.'

'But—'

Jennet placed a finger to his lips. 'I don't want to talk about my mother. There's something else I'd far rather do.'

He smiled and drew her close. 'Me too.'

They kissed, and then she pulled away to lift herself up and bend over him. Slowly, she began to drag the tips of her breasts across his chest, circling and moving. As she skimmed her nipples across his, Connor made a noise of satisfaction deep in his throat.

'You like that?' she asked.

'I like everything you do to me.'

Holding her breasts firm in her hands, she rubbed them over the brown discs of his nipples again. Harder this time. And again, in deliberately tantalising strokes. He groaned. Smiling, she moved lower, circling her breasts over his chest and the plane of his stomach, in a way which excited both of them.

'And I like that,' she murmured as she reached his thighs.

'Heaven be praised.' He put his hand on the top of her head, guiding her closer to his arousal. 'Please,' he said.

She kissed the swollen tip, licking away a diamond drop.

'This is pure torment,' he said as her moist caresses continued.

His body shuddered and when she looked up she saw that his colour had darkened and his fists were clenched. She felt a heady rush of emotion. She had not realised she possessed the power to disturb him so deeply and it thrilled her.

'Remember I boasted of my control?' he said, his lips parted in gasping breaths. 'I lied.'

Taking hold of her shoulders, he drew her up and—a moment later—she straddled him. Their thighs interlocked and as she sat above him he reached for her breasts. His fingers stroked, rubbed, pinched. Her hips moved. A rhythm began. She stretched an arm down and backwards, her fingers cupping and cradling between his legs.

'Yes,' Connor said, in a harsh voice. The rhythm moved into a wild, primitive tempo which neither of them could control. 'Yes, yes...*yes*!'

Afterwards he fell quickly asleep, but Jennet lay awake. The evening had been so good, she brooded, until her mother had arrived. She resented her visit. She knew there was no malice in her flirting and yet she felt angry with her for fluttering her lashes at Connor and for making him laugh. Perhaps she was being unfair and irrational, but—

Losing patience, she slid from the bed and pulled on a light pastel blue robe. Sleep would be impossible unless she cleared her thoughts from her head. Quietly opening the French windows, she walked out onto the terrace. A round melon moon shone high in the sky and the garden was patterned in silver light and black shadow.

Her mother would only be here for a couple of days, she reflected. She could manage two days. She *had* to manage.

'Moon-gazing?' Connor enquired, and she turned to see him standing on his crutches in the doorway of the French windows.

She gave a wan smile. 'Yes.'

'Were you keen on Mitch?' he enquired, swinging outside. 'Did you love him?'

'Heavens, no! He seemed nice enough, but I barely knew him.'

'But his relationship with your mother is the reason why you refused to write a toyboy romance for *Hutton's Spa*?'

'That relationship, and others.' Jennet tightened the sash of her robe. 'In recent years Tina's developed a liking for younger and younger men.'

'How old is this Mitch?' he asked.

'Twenty-eight, so the gap's nearer to thirty years than twenty.'

'He's younger than you,' Connor observed. 'And you thought their relationship was "icky"?'

'Yes. Yet they were happy while it lasted and the age difference didn't appear to bother either of them, so why should it bother me?'

'Because she's your mother. You may be accepting of her, but you don't approve of her,' he said.

'No, I don't. When I think about her I feel such a cocktail of emotions. We love each other and she's proud of me, always pleased for me, can be so generous—yet I don't trust her. We're close and I feel protective, but she's also—' She broke off to tilt her head. A key was turning in a lock. 'Russ is home.'

'I'll go and tell him that your mother's sleeping upstairs,' he said, and swung out.

When they returned to bed Connor soon fell asleep again and, as he turned, he stretched his arm over her in the dark. Jennet felt a pang. At the restaurant she had told him that she liked him, but she had a suspicion that her liking came alarmingly closer to love. Lifting his arm from her, she rolled away and onto her side. An essential factor in her appeal to him was that she would make no attempt to tie him down—so loving him was pointless.

CHAPTER EIGHT

'THANKS for everything. It's been a pleasure and a privilege to stay with the composer who penned those immortal words—' Russ broke into song '—"If you want your taste buds—"'

'Can it,' Jennet said, laughing.

'And I look forward to us getting together again when I return home in a couple of months' time.'

'Mmm,' she replied, being vague and noncommittal.

It was ten o'clock the next morning. A bulging rucksack stood on the doorstep, a taxi was expected, and Russ, clad in twill shirt and shorts, sneakers and a back-to-front baseball cap, had launched into thanks and goodbyes. Last night he and the girls had agreed to join forces and today they were setting off on their way up into Switzerland.

'Behave yourself and don't forget to ring,' Connor instructed.

His son groaned. 'The guy never lets up. No, Dad. The cab will come?' he said, looking anxiously at his watch. 'The ferry leaves in fifty minutes.'

'It'll be here soon,' she assured him, 'and you have plenty of time.'

The tip-tap of stiletto heels sounded on the ceramic floor of the hallway.

'Made it,' Tina said, joining them. She pressed a wad of notes into Russ's hand. 'A few lire to buy a treat or two on your journey.'

An hour ago when the three of them had had breakfast, the newest arrival had stayed in bed. Although yesterday's travelling had meant a long day, she never rose early and when she did surface she did so leisurely. She took her time choosing what to wear, fixing her hair and applying her make-up.

The time had been well spent for, in an ivory linen shift and with her silvery blonde hair caught on top of her head in a bundle with long wisps trailing down, she looked china-doll pretty and stylish. A darn sight more stylish than she was in an outsized coral T-shirt worn over faded cut-offs with denim strings dangling down her legs and with her face scrubbed clean, Jennet thought ruefully.

Russ grinned. 'Thanks very much—er—Tina, isn't it?'

'Tina Lemoine,' his benefactor said, with a gracious smile. 'It must've been quite a surprise for you to bump into me on the landing this morning.'

'No, I knew Jennet's mum was here.'

There was a curling of brows and a tinkle of semi-protesting laughter. 'Jennet's *mum*?'

'The name Tina Lemoine doesn't mean anything to him,' Connor explained.

Tina frowned, torn between modesty and a wish to make it clear how famous she was. Her need to be the star won.

'I used to go around with The Sloop,' she announced, as if this information would cause goggle eyes and a clamouring for her autograph.

'The Sloop?' Russ turned down his mouth. 'They're way past their sell-by date. A load of old codgers in my—' He stopped. He had seen her expression. 'I often bump into people on the landing in the morning,' he carried on, in a hasty, frantic and transparent attempt to rescue himself. 'Either my little sisters or my mother. Not that you remind me of my mother. She's much plumper than you and nowhere near as smart.' Tina started to smile. 'Mum's younger, too,' he added guilelessly. 'A lot younger.'

The smile froze. 'I shall have breakfast,' she declared, and tip-tapped away.

A few moments later, the taxi appeared. Russ swung the heavy rucksack onto his shoulder and there was a round of final goodbyes.

'I apologise for my son's big mouth,' Connor said as they waved the taxi away.

Jennet grinned. Whilst she had no wish to be uncharitable, she had found the incident amusing.

'He was only being honest.'

'True. Mind you,' he went on, 'Tina looks fantastic for her age and is great entertainment value.'

She nodded, but said nothing. After less than twelve hours, she was already suffering from a bad case of mother fatigue, she thought as they went indoors.

'Are you two still intending to work today?' Tina enquired, looking in from the terrace where, having broken off from kiwi fruit, muesli and coffee, she had gone to smoke her first cigarette. 'All day?'

'I am,' she said.

'And me,' Connor confirmed.

'Then I shall sunbathe,' the visitor declared, in the voice of a martyr.

'And make notes for your autobiography?' Jennet enquired warily.

'No, no, I'm on holiday. And because I am I insist that, on the dot of five, we all go into town and enjoy Happy Hour at one of the hotels.' Tina went to lift the telephone. 'If you tell me the number, I shall fix a cab now.'

Jennet sighed. She would far rather relax at the villa than sit in a bar, but after a day alone her mother would be desperate for a change of scene—if not chewing the carpet.

A cab was ordered and they dispersed.

In the kitchen, Jennet read through her draft, made a couple of alterations and inserted a clean sheet of paper into her portable typewriter. Concentrating took time, but gradually the inspiration began to flow.

She stopped to prepare rolls for a snack lunch which they ate on the terrace, and returned to work. Now the dialogue was coming smoothly, so smoothly that when she reached a break in the action, around four o'clock, she decided to finish. Tina had been complaining of boredom at lunchtime, so she would take pity on her.

Tidying away her writing paraphernalia, she went out onto the terrace. The lounger positioned beneath the large umbrella lay empty. There was no sign of the sunbather. Had she gone for a solitary walk? It seemed out of character. Jennet shot a wry glance at the upstairs window. A more likely explanation for her absence would be that she had already started on the primping and perfecting considered necessary for their foray into town.

Returning indoors, she made for the hall and the flight of stone steps which led down to the cellar. She would see how Connor was progressing with his painting. As she approached the door, which stood open, she heard the murmur of voices. The missing person had been located. Jennet started down the steps in her soft-soled espadrilles—and stopped, her eyes travelling to the far corner of the low-ceilinged room. Connor had his arm around her mother, who, wearing a flowered bikini and high heeled mules, was smiling up at him.

Her heart cramped. A fuse seemed to blow in her brain. She wheeled round, sped back into the hall and straight up the staircase to her room. Connor—*her* lover—had succumbed to Tina's charms! OK, he might not be about to hop into bed with her, but to some degree he had been captivated. She felt the hot smack of anger. How could he? How dared he? Why must he be like every other stupidly impressionable man?

She wanted to strangle him, Jennet thought fiercely. She wanted to rant and rail, and smash plates. Instead, she flung open the wardrobe door and took out a black on white polka-dot dress. It had cap sleeves, a low, boat-shaped neck and a short fluted skirt which flounced around her legs when she walked. It was a come-hither dress. A sexy dress. She would play her mother at her own game. She would bat her eyelids, coo and simper, act the siren!

She changed, fastened on strappy sandals and brushed her hair. She shaved her legs and re-lacquered her nails, fingers and toes, in pearly Tropical Sunrise. She made up her face, using a sultry kohl pencil around her eyes, and sprayed a musky perfume onto pulse points and into her cleavage. White hoops were pinned in her ears and a white bangle clasped around her wrist.

Her hands on her hips, Jennet gazed defiantly at the *femme fatale* whom she saw in the mirror.

'Go get him, girl!' she instructed, and stalked downstairs.

Her companions were waiting for her. Connor's painting T-shirt and shorts had been replaced by a blue and white striped poplin shirt and pale trousers, while Tina looked a vision of elegance in her ivory shift.

When he saw her, her prey pursed his lips in a low whistle.

'Nice?' she enquired, performing a pirouette which sent the polka-dot dress fluttering out around her thighs.

Connor growled.

'Isn't my daughter just too exquisite for words?' her mother said, placing a hand on his arm.

His gaze stayed on Jennet. 'Indeed she is,' he replied.

Stepping between them, she removed the slender fingers and replaced them with her own. 'Hands off, Mom, this is my man,' she said chirpily, and leaned close against him. 'Aren't you?'

Humour glinted in his eyes. 'Now and for always,' he vowed.

'You called me Mom,' Tina said, with a little *moue* of protest.

'You'd prefer Ma or Mummy?' she enquired. 'But why shouldn't I? You are my mother and you're plenty old enough to be a grandmother.'

She knew that playing the age card was unfair, but Tina's vamping was unfair too. One way and another, it had wreaked havoc over the years.

'But a glamorous granny,' Connor said gallantly.

The older woman pouted, thought better of it, and pouted again. She seemed uncertain how to react.

'Can't have you looking untidy,' Jennet declared, and, reaching up both hands, she tugged at his perfectly neat collar.

'Thanks,' he said.

She smiled into his eyes and, in a provocative gesture, drew the tip of her finger down the exposed V of his throat until it reached the top button. 'Any time,' she said huskily.

Her mother had been watching and frowning, but, as a horn tooted outside, she hurried over to the door. 'The cab's arrived,' she reported, and swept outside.

'Ya-boo sucks to her and the first round to you,' Connor said, his mouth crooked with amusement. 'This is going to be one hell of an evening.'

'Meaning?'

'Two beautiful women fighting over me—it's every man's dream. What's your next move—to slither all over me?' He moaned in mock anguish. 'I can hardly wait. OK if I go and install myself in the cab while you lock up?' he enquired.

She nodded. 'Do.'

As he swung off on his crutches, Jennet eyed his tall figure. She was damned if she would give him the satisfaction of competing for his attentions, she thought suddenly, even though she knew she would win—which appealed to her female vanity. Besides, trading eyelash flutter for eyelash flutter—with her *mother*, for heaven's sakes!—was tacky. She put a higher value on herself.

And what was the point? Connor might have claimed to be hers 'now and for always', but in two weeks' time their personal relationship ended. Pain twisted inside her heart. It had been agreed.

She looked at the cab where her mother was in the back seat, leaning forward to speak to Connor who had sat beside the driver. She did not want to go to a bar and she would *not* go, she thought rebelliously. To hell with Happy Hour—and to hell with both of them!

As the driver revved his engine, she went to speak to him through his open window.

'I'm not coming. It's just two.'

'*Va bene,*' he replied, with a shrug which acknowledged the waywardness of women, and accelerated away.

Powering back to the front door, Jennet slammed it shut behind her and marched through the house. She went out of the French windows and down the garden. Pink and white oleander bushes marked the haphazard boundary and she ploughed through them and into the fields. She did not care where she was going. All that mattered was getting away.

She needed to get away from Connor, she thought as she stopped briefly to take off her sandals. Living with him, sleeping with him, making love for two more weeks would be too painful. Agony. She would ring the airline and ask for her return ticket to be switched to tomorrow, she decided, tramping through the long grass. And, whilst working on *Hutton's Spa* necessitated their continued contact, she would keep it to the minimum and do her damnedest to make sure they were never, ever alone.

Jennet halted, meaning to set off back, then sank down in the shade of an olive tree. She couldn't depart tomorrow. Life was not that simple. Before she went, beds needed to be stripped down, personal possessions locked away in an 'owner's' cupboard and the villa left tidy for future visitors. She could not walk out when there were other people in residence. She scrunched up her pearly-varnished toes. And did she want to leave Connor in the villa with her mother?

'Jennet!'

Peering back around the tree, she saw Connor slaloming towards her down the field on his crutches. She skewered him with a glare. The traitor had come to find her.

'What are you playing at, deserting us like—like that?' he panted as he hop-swung nearer.

'I'm not playing at anything,' she retorted, anger catapulting her to her feet. 'It's *you* who's— Careful!' she warned, when he skidded and seemed about to fall. 'Though why should I care about you?' she enquired as he steadied himself. 'Care about what you do? I don't. You're a free agent and you can do whatever you damn well choose.' Her nostrils flared. 'However, I wish you didn't have to be so *bloody* predictable!'

He came to a stop beside her. 'Predictable?'

'I thought you had some sense. I thought you had... calibre. I never thought you'd let me down.' Without warning, thick tears were clotting her throat, but she choked them back. She would not cry over him, she would *not*. 'I believed that for the short time of our holiday romance you'd be true to me.'

Connor frowned. Her mouth had trembled and her green eyes looked huge and sad and suspiciously watery. 'You're upset,' he said.

Jennet sniffed. 'A for observation,' she snapped.

'But, sorry, I don't know what you're talking about.'

'I saw you in the cellar.'

'The cellar?' he asked.

'A sudden memory loss has hit?' Her laugh was pure disdain. 'How convenient!'

His eyes narrowed. 'You saw me down there with your mother?'

'I did. But save the apologies because, frankly, I don't give a—'

'I'm not apologising.'

'No?' She gave an offhand shrug. 'Your choice.'

'Because her own company bores her stiff Tina came down to chat and, as she seems prone to do, somewhere during the conversation she placed her hand on my arm.' His tone was brusque and the delivery clipped. 'However, she'd neglected to remember that I was standing on one leg. I wobbled, she wobbled because she totters around in those stupidly high heels, and in order to remain upright I latched an arm around her. It seemed preferable to falling onto the can of paint. Then she proceeded to eye-bat up to around ten on the Richter scale and thank me for saving *her*.'

'She told you what a rugged, virile, handsome, helpful hunk you were?'

'You guessed. However, I was not having my wicked way with her. Nor would I ever feel the slightest inclination to do so, because she leaves me cold.' His voice cracked like a whip. 'Stone-cold.'

Jennet felt a thankful swoop of relief. 'You're not attracted to her?'

'No. Do you want it in writing? You can have it in writing, in triplicate, or etched on marble. The only woman who attracts me is you, which I thought I'd been making abundantly clear. And now I shall have to sit down.'

'Tina went on into town?' she enquired, sitting beside him as he lowered himself onto the grass.

'No, she's waiting at the villa. She realised you were mad at her for flirting—'

'She realised it'd upset someone? That's the first time ever.'

'And she does care about you.'

'Yes.' The green of her eyes darkened. 'Though caring for me didn't keep her from flirting with you and it never stopped her flirting with Stuart.'

'It's flirting by numbers,' Connor said dismissively. 'She's been doing it for so long that it's become automatic, a force of habit. It doesn't demonstrate attraction. She doesn't give a monkey's who the guy is, the only criterion is that he's male. I know it, you know it and your husband would've known it too.'

She shook her head. 'He took it for real.'

'He believed your mother fancied him?'

'More than that.' Jennet stared straight ahead. The sordid secret had festered inside her like a malignancy for so long, but now she had to tell him. She wanted to tell him the things which she had sworn she would never reveal. She *needed* to tell him. She drew in a shaky breath. 'Stuart swore she'd have sex with him if he asked. That's what we were arguing about on the night that he was killed.'

'Oh, God,' he said, in a stricken voice.

'Remember I told you how the couple had boasted about the yacht they kept in Spain?' she asked, turning to him. 'They said they'd gone cruising with another younger couple and indicated, by winks and innu-endoes, that there'd been wife-swapping. During the evening, the man'd made it obvious that he liked me and when we were alone for a few minutes—his wife had dragged Stuart off to show him the swimming pool—he told me that I was the reason he'd asked us to dinner. Apparently he'd seen me around and thought I was...juicy.'

'And he hoped you and your husband might indulge in some wife-swapping too?'

'He didn't say it outright, but he suggested we should join them in Spain some time during the next couple of months and "let rip". When we left I told Stuart I thought the couple were obnoxious and said there was no way I'd ever set foot on their boat.' She moistened her lips. 'He called me a spoilsport.'

'He didn't want to go?' Connor protested.

'He said we should consider the invitation, but he'd have run a mile if the woman, who was a strident bottle-blonde, had put her hand on his knee. I told him not to be so silly, at which point he announced that he couldn't understand how someone like me could have such a go-for-it mother. He said Tina wouldn't turn up her nose at group sex nor at going to bed with him. He declared that since the first time he'd seen her it'd been on his mind.'

Connor put his arm around her shoulders. 'Jen,' he said, in soft sympathy.

'I was appalled . . . and disgusted . . . and I felt so betrayed. I thought Stuart'd married me because he loved me, but it seemed as if he'd married me because he was lusting after my mother. It was as if the world had shattered.' Tears were stinging at the back of her eyes. 'He'd demolished our relationship and trashed me. I mean, why did he want to have sex with her? Wasn't I satisfying him? I'd always believed our love life was OK, but—'

'Just OK?' Connor asked.

'Just OK. It wasn't like it is between us.' She managed a faint smile. 'A many-splendoured thing. I'd always imagined that Stuart had far more . . . value than my mother's lightweight men,' she continued, 'but what he'd said made him just like them. My immediate reaction was blinding anger, but then I started to shake and I wanted to be sick.

'I told him that even if he fancied Tina she didn't fancy him, but he insisted I was wrong. He said she'd made it clear that she lusted after him—' her voice cracked and suddenly she was crying, but she kept on talking '—and as he walked off along the road he yelled back that I was to go to hell and that he and Tina would be dynamite in bed.'

'It was the wine talking,' Connor declared, lifting a hip to take a handkerchief from his trouser pocket and pass it to her.

'You think so?' she asked as she blew her nose.

'For certain. You said he'd had more than usual and it'd made him belligerent and given him false courage. But he didn't mean what he was saying—any of it.'

Jennet looked at him with hesitant green eyes. 'No?'

'No. You know how people can sometimes accuse others of their own deficiencies in an attempt to switch the blame and protect themselves?' he enquired.

She nodded. 'Yes.'

'It seems to me that the reason your husband hit out and rubbished you was because, deep down, he'd become aware of his own inhibitions. And because he felt inadequate he attacked you.'

She frowned. Her horror of reliving the dreadful night meant she had never analysed Stuart's outburst, but all of a sudden his motivation—though twisted—seemed obvious.

'That makes sense,' she agreed. 'I never suggested that he wasn't exactly an adventurous lover, but he must've suspected it.'

'So every word he said was complete bravado and utter drivel. Right?' Connor demanded.

She smiled. She trusted him, his wisdom and his judgement, and she recognised that he spoke the truth. 'Right.' A moment later, her smile faded. 'But even though I know that, now, the jogger doesn't know it.'

'You mean the guy who witnessed the accident?'

'Yes. If he should discover that I'm Tina Lemoine's daughter, he'll realise that the Tina whom Stuart was shouting about was his mother-in-law. And, as seems to be the way of things these days, he could decide to sell his story to the newspapers.'

His dark brows lowered. 'This is why you were so scared of being photographed by the guy from *The Comet*?'

Jennet bobbed her head. 'I thought he wanted a picture for the "find Tina's daughter" campaign, in which case if the jogger had seen it he would've made the connection. It's the risk of him seeing me and recognising me that makes me nervous about appearing on television. And why I don't want my mother to write her book, though the book could hurt other people too. But if Stuart's claims were splashed all over the tabloids...' She shuddered. 'Everyone would snigger about them and for the rest of my life I'd feel ... grubby and pointed at.'

'It'd be grim,' Connor agreed, and fell silent, thinking. 'Didn't you say that the jogger hadn't heard the Mercedes?'

'That's what he told me.'

'Why didn't he hear it? Was he too far away?'

'No, he was jogging down the road towards us and because it was midnight it was quiet. Why? What difference does it make?' she asked.

'It could make a big difference,' he said slowly. 'If, as joggers often do, the guy was listening to a personal stereo, then—'

Her mind flew back over the years. 'He was,' she said, in an awed, wondering, disbelieving voice. She looked at him, a smile spreading across her face. 'Connor, he was! I remember now, he had earphones around his neck and a cassette player clipped to his waist. When he bent down to Stuart, the cassette tumbled off and he pushed it into his pockct.'

'Which is why he didn't hear the car and—' He broke off. 'Stuart was shouting back at you?'

'Back over his shoulder, away from the jogger,' she said.

'And why the guy couldn't have heard your quarrel.'

She gave her head a little shake. 'Why didn't I realise that?'

'Because you were in shock. Deep shock.'

'But for three years I've lived in fear and dread, and it was all for nothing,' Jennet said, and her lower lip quivered and the tears started afresh.

'Sweetheart,' Connor said.

He put his arms around her and she laid her head on his shoulder and cried. She cried with relief—relief that Stuart's claims would never be exposed to the glare of the media and with relief from, at last, having shared her secret. Shared it with a man of compassion.

She pressed closer. Connor felt firm and strong. His arms were a haven, a place of comfort and safety. For the first time in a very long time, she felt protected. She had a sense of belonging, which made no sense at all.

'I'm here,' he murmured, as if he knew what she was thinking, and she nodded wordlessly through her tears.

Gradually, the sobs lessened and she blew her nose again. 'Afterwards I lost all my confidence,' Jennet continued, purging herself and determined to finish her story, 'and became very introspective. I felt a complete failure. But I'm one of life's survivors—'

'A toughie,' he said, gently cuffing her chin with his knuckles.

'—and in time I pulled myself together and started to feel good about myself again.' She looked at him with wet, spiky-lashed eyes. 'I thought the wounds had healed, but now I realise that all I did was smother them in bandages. I was in denial, as the shrinks say. When you talked of putting a younger man/older woman romance into *Hutton's Spa*, it threw me,' she said. 'Writing it would've forced me to think about what Stuart had said and—' she paused, her face tightening '—made me wonder if it was true.'

'Meaning that Tina might've slept with him—if he'd suggested it, which he would never've done?' Connor shook his head. 'No way.'

'I'm not so sure. She has a very casual attitude towards sex and maybe if the time and the place had been right—' Jennet rose to her feet. 'We'd better go back. She'll be wondering where we are.'

When they returned to the villa, her mother was pacing anxiously up and down the terrace with a cigarette in her hand. Beside her, on a low table, an ashtray was full of stubs.

'You forgive me?' Tina demanded.

She nodded. 'I do.'

'Thank goodness,' the older woman declared, hugging her. 'I love you so much and I don't want to hurt you or to annoy you. I don't know what I'd do if we ever fell out.'

'So you won't be mauling me again?' Connor enquired.

Tina's beauty and playfulness masked a woman whom, whilst she was curiously endearing, he considered to be little more than a spoilt child. Her careless behaviour had played a pivotal role in Jennet's distress and she had a lot to answer for. It was high time she thought about the consequences of her actions and became more responsible.

'Maul?' Tina queried.

He was smiling, and yet the idea made her feel uneasy.

'If a man of fifty-odd went around touching members of the opposite sex like you do, it'd be called sexual harassment. I assume you wouldn't want to hurt Silvio's wife, either?' he continued.

'Of course not.'

'But by coming on to her husband you do hurt her.'

'She hates it,' Jennet said.

Her mother inhaled slowly, the end of her filter-tip glowing red. All of a sudden, she had a lot to think about.

'When I leave tomorrow, I shall return to Portugal,' she declared.

'Good idea,' Connor said, and they sat down. 'We've just been discussing the idea of an older woman who has a...liaison with her son-in-law.'

Jennet shot him a horrified look. She knew he could be blunt, but he must not be *this* blunt.

'Connor, I don't—' she started.

'Someone suggested it for *Hutton's Spa*,' he went on calmly. 'The woman's an attractive type who likes to party and—'

'I don't care who she is,' Tina cut in, with a curl of her lip. 'No one with the least integrity or feeling would ever do something so distasteful.'

'My view too,' he said, and raised his brows at Jennet. 'This book which you're thinking of writing,' he went on. 'Is it worth the effort?'

'What do you mean?' the would-be author enquired.

'Call me old-fashioned, but it seems to me that before anyone writes their autobiography they ought to have accomplished something special, like climbing Everest, or excelled in a particular field. Have you?'

There was a pout. 'No, but I can tell some interesting stories about people I've met.'

'Several of whom were lovers? So, in essence, your book would be yet another kiss-and-tell?'

Jennet watched on with interest. Her mother was listening intently to Connor who was giving the kind of firm male guidance which her own father had once given and which Tina respected.

'I suppose so,' Tina conceded, and frowned. 'But a kiss-and-tell would be—'

'Icky?' he suggested, sliding a look in Jennet's direction.

'Right. So what do I do with my spare time?' his disciple enquired.

'You find yourself a job.'

The older woman's brows soared. She had not worked for thirty years and then she had only played at working.

'A job?' she protested.

'You speak Portuguese?' The silver-blonde head nodded. 'Then you could be a tour guide or a holiday rep. An attractive woman like you shouldn't have too much difficulty finding that kind of work.'

'I'll try it!' Tina declared, and began talking excitedly about people she knew who might help her, offices she could call into, even other ideas for gainful employment.

'Now it's time to ring for a cab to take you into town,' Connor said as she wound down.

'Just me?'

'I'm sure you can find someone to chat to and—' he reached out to take hold of Jennet's hand '—I would like to spend some time alone with this exquisite lady.'

'I shall have dinner out,' Tina decided, when a cab had been ordered. 'There's a nice restaurant around the corner from the church which has a rather dishy head waiter—'

'And you're going to make eyes at him?' he enquired.

The older woman roared with laughter. 'Yes, but I promise not to maul. Don't wait up for me.'

'She isn't going to change,' Jennet said, when her mother had gone and they were sitting on the sofa on the terrace, sipping wine and watching the setting sun cast long shadows across the garden.

'No, though with luck she'll be a little more circumspect in future.'

'Thank you for raising the son-in-law question. I was shocked when you did—and terrified.'

'I know,' he said. 'But I reckoned that if the answer was as you feared you'd have lost nothing. And if it wasn't—'

'I'd gain peace of mind. Which I have. Now I can put the past behind me in total, thanks to you.'

'I'm pleased to have been able to help,' Connor said. He looked at her. 'But what about the future?'

'The future?'

'Our future. You were furious when it seemed as if you'd caught me in a clinch with Tina in the cellar, but you also wanted to cry. You cared so much that you were on the point of crying—over me.'

Jennet flashed a smile. 'A silly moment,' she claimed.

'No,' he said, shaking his head. 'You remember how I told you I was going to sleep with you every night and you said you understood? You didn't. The reason I wanted to sleep with you was because I wanted to make you realise how deeply I care about you.'

'You care deeply?' she asked, feeling a wild flare of hope, but warning herself to keep cool and not to jump to any conclusions. 'But you said we should treat our stay here as a holiday romance—'

'And you said we should forget it when we returned home and revert to our working relationship.'

She frowned. 'That's what you wanted.'

'No. I was going to suggest that when we got back we should decide what we thought about each other and take the relationship from there. And I hoped that by that time you'd have realised we were ideally matched in all departments and would've decided you couldn't live without me.'

A breathless exhilaration snatched the air from her lungs. 'Couldn't live—live without you?' Jennet asked jerkily.

Connor stretched out a hand, taking hold of hers and drawing her along the sofa until she was sitting close beside him. 'When you told me that you were going to sleep with me, you also asked if I understood. I did, but again you didn't. At least, I don't think so.'

'Could you put that into plain English?'

'You wanted us to spend every night together because you love me.'

She swallowed. 'I do,' she admitted.

'And I love you.' He cast a wry look at his plaster. 'It's going to be tricky going down on one knee, so would you mind if we skip that bit?' He entwined her fingers with his. 'Please will you marry me?'

'But what about your freedom? And hating to be tied down? And not being husband material?'

'That was before we came to Capri. And ever since we did I've been fighting a losing battle. Yes or no?' he demanded.

'Yes, yes, *yes*,' Jennet said, and she kissed him.

'Your mother told us not to wait up,' he said as they came up for air a few minutes later, 'so how's about we go to bed?'

'Now? And get up later for dinner?'

Connor grinned, the grooves deepening in his cheeks. 'If we feel inclined.'

The sun set, darkness fell—and it was the next morning before they arose.

CHAPTER NINE

FLASH bulbs popped, dazzled. Television cameras whirred. The people at the round dinner tables which filled the grandly chandeliered and thick-carpeted function room applauded. Smiling at the man who stood on the platform, Jennet clapped loudly. She was tempted to put two fingers in her mouth and give a piercing whistle, but decided that, for someone wearing a long, sophisticated slim white dress and who had her hair twisted into a chic, polished coil, it would be unladylike.

Connor had been presented with his Best Director trophy, had replied with a short speech of thanks and was now receiving the acclaim of fellow members of the television industry. She had gone through the same happy procedure a few minutes earlier.

As he came down from the stage and threaded his way back through the white-damask-clothed tables, she watched him. That morning his second plaster cast had been removed and now he walked with a cane. It was a silver-handled ebony cane, specially bought to go with his black tuxedo. Her heartbeat quickened. In the evening clothes, he looked so dashing and handsome.

'Yet another prize,' Lester crowed as Connor resumed his seat beside her at the Ensign table. Champagne flowed and there was more delighted praise from their colleagues.

'In your acceptance speech you thanked Jennet. "Without whom *Hutton's Spa* would never've happened", and in hers she thanked you "without whom

Hutton's Spa would never've been such a success,"' the chairman remarked, and grinned. 'Sounded like a mutual admiration society.'

'It is,' Connor agreed, sliding a hand beneath the table and squeezing her knee. 'And we're a mutual support team.'

'After *Hutton's Spa*, you'll write the airline six-parter,' Lester went on, turning to her. 'Any ideas for a production after that?'

Jennet smiled. 'A baby.'

'Or two or three,' Connor said.

Eileen Sewell, who was a plump, friendly, grey-haired woman, admired the diamond solitaire which sparkled on the third finger of Jennet's left hand. 'Have you fixed a date for your wedding?'

'We're getting married in six weeks' time,' she told her.

'And we hope you and Lester will be there,' Connor said.

'You bet we will,' the chairman declared. 'Couldn't miss watching the tiger being tamed.'

'Tiger?' Jennet laughed. 'I reckon he's just a big pussycat.'

'And now the beaver has something more than her writing to be eager about,' Connor said, smiling at her. He crooked a brow. 'Yes?'

'Oh, yes,' she agreed.

'Where are you going to live?' Lester asked. 'In Hammersmith or down in Sussex?'

'To begin with we'll stay at my apartment during the week,' Connor told him, 'and spend our weekends at Jennet's. But after a year or so we plan to sell both places and buy a family house in the country but closer to London.'

A call of 'Done it again' from a nearby table broke into the conversation and had everyone turning to see that executives from a rival television company were raising their glasses.

'Con, you and I'd better go and have a drink with the opposition, the losers,' Lester said, chuckling.

'You mean let's go and gloat?' he asked drily.

'Why not? That's what these occasions are for.'

As the two men excused themselves and disappeared, and as music started up in the adjoining ballroom, Eileen Sewell moved to sit next to Jennet.

'I believe you and Connor were in Capri recently. Did you manage to get to the Blue Grotto?' she enquired.

'We did. We went everywhere,' Jennet said, and told her of the places they had visited and what they had done.

With her draft finished and Connor's painting completed, they had spent the last week exploring the island and sampling its delights.

They had admired the mosaics and bronze heads in the Villa of San Michele, eaten *sfogliatelle*, a sweet pastry stuffed with ricotta and candied fruit, marvelled at the tiny church of St Michael Archangel in Ana Capri with its inlaid Garden of Eden tiled floor. They had browsed in sophisticated shopping malls—and treated themselves to Italian designer shirts, gone on boat trips around the island, sampled the local lemon liqueur, taken the funicular railway from the Marina Grande to the Piazzetta.

And every evening after their sightseeing—and sometimes in between—they had made love, which, because they were secure in their love for each other, had been a blending of spirits as well as bodies.

'Would you like to dance?' Connor asked her, when he and Lester returned.

The rock 'n roll music which had been coming from the ballroom had changed to a slow, smoochy melody and the lights had dimmed.

'Will you be able to manage?' Jennet enquired. 'You're still wearing a bandage and the consultant did say to take care for a while.'

'I can manage.' He gave a lopsided grin. 'So long as I have you to hold onto.'

'It's strange,' she reflected as they swayed together with arms wrapped around each other. 'For the first twelve months, I never really *noticed* you.'

'That's because you'd been hurt and you were frightened of being hurt again. But in time you recovered and were ready to notice a man again.'

She arched a teasing brow. 'And because you were unattached, in close proximity and blessed with a healthy sex drive the man just happened to be you?'

'I don't think it was that random,' he protested.

'You mean it could've been written in the stars?'

Connor drew her closer. 'In capital letters. And now we're together to love and to cherish, until death us do part. Understand?'

Jennet smiled into the grey eyes which were eloquent with love. 'I understand,' she said.

MILLS & BOON®

Next Month's Romances

♡

Each month you can choose from a wide variety of romance novels from Mills & Boon. Below are the new titles to look out for next month from the Presents and Enchanted series.

Presents™

SEDUCING THE ENEMY	Emma Darcy
WILDEST DREAMS	Carole Mortimer
A TYPICAL MALE!	Sally Wentworth
SETTLING THE SCORE	Sharon Kendrick
ACCIDENTAL MISTRESS	Cathy Williams
A HUSBAND FOR THE TAKING	Amanda Browning
BOOTS IN THE BEDROOM!	Alison Kelly
A MARRIAGE IN THE MAKING	Natalie Fox

Enchanted™

THE NINETY-DAY WIFE	Emma Goldrick
COURTING TROUBLE	Patricia Wilson
TWO-PARENT FAMILY	Patricia Knoll
BRIDE FOR HIRE	Jessica Hart
REBEL WITHOUT A BRIDE	Catherine Leigh
RACHEL'S CHILD	Jennifer Taylor
TEMPORARY TEXAN	Heather Allison
THIS MAN AND THIS WOMAN	Lucy Gordon

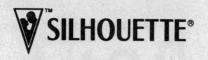
™SILHOUETTE®

Tempting...Tantalising...Terrifying!

Strangers
in the night

Three spooky love stories in one compelling
volume by three masters of the genre:

Dark Journey by Anne Stuart
Catching Dreams by Chelsea Quinn Yarbro
Beyond Twilight by Maggie Shayne

Available: July 1997   Price: £4.99

New York Times bestselling author
of *Class Reunion*

RONA
JAFFE

The COUSINS

**A sweeping saga of family loyalties and
disloyalties, choices and compromises,
destruction and survival.**

"Rona Jaffe's storytelling is irresistible."
—Los Angeles Times

"...a page-turner all the way."
—Cosmopolitan

MIRA®

AVAILABLE IN PAPERBACK
FROM JUNE 1997

SUMMER SEARCH

How would you like to win a year's supply of Mills & Boon®
books? Well you can and they're FREE! Simply complete the
competition below and send it to us by 31st December 1997.
The first five correct entries picked after the closing date will
each win a year's subscription to the Mills & Boon series of
their choice. What could be easier?

SPADE
SUNSHINE
PICNIC
BEACHBALL
SWIMMING
SUNBATHING
CLOUDLESS
FUN
TOWEL
SAND
HOLIDAY

W	Q	T	U	H	S	P	A	D	E	M	B
E	Q	R	U	O	T	T	K	I	U	I	E
N	B	G	H	L	H	G	O	D	W	K	A
I	I	O	A	I	N	E	S	W	Q	L	C
H	N	U	N	D	D	F	W	P	E	O	H
S	U	N	B	A	T	H	I	N	G	L	B
N	S	E	A	Y	F	C	M	D	A	R	A
U	B	P	K	A	N	D	M	N	U	T	L
S	E	N	L	I	Y	B	I	A	N	U	L
H	B	U	C	K	E	T	N	S	N	U	E
T	A	E	W	T	O	H	G	H	O	T	F
C	L	O	U	D	L	E	S	S	P	W	N

C7F

Please turn over for details of how to enter ☞

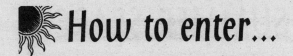# How to enter...

Hidden in the grid are eleven different summer related words. You'll find the list beside the word puzzle overleaf and they can be read backwards, forwards, up, down and diagonally. As you find each word, circle it or put a line through it. When you have found all eleven, don't forget to fill in your name and address in the space provided below and pop this page in an envelope (you don't even need a stamp) and post it today. Hurry competition ends 31st December 1997.

Mills & Boon Summer Search Competition
FREEPOST, Croydon, Surrey, CR9 3WZ
EIRE readers send competition to PO Box 4546, Dublin 24.

Please tick the series you would like to receive if you are a winner
Presents™ ❏   Enchanted™ ❏   Temptation® ❏
Medical Romance™ ❏   Historical Romance™ ❏

Are you a Reader Service™ Subscriber?   Yes ❏   No ❏

Ms/Mrs/Miss/Mr _____
                                              (BLOCK CAPS PLEASE)

Address _____

_____

_____ Postcode _____

(I am over 18 years of age)